PRAISE FOR *PHILISTEENS*

'In the great first-person retrospective approaches of Padgett Powell's Simons
Manigault in *Edisto*, or Dale Ray Phillips's Richard in *My People's Waltz*,
Steve Lambert offers us Neil—both naive and knowing—slyly meandering
through bullies, skateboarders, cohorts, teasers, rednecks, punk rockers,
losers, haters, slackers, and fatalists. *Philisteens* is a *romp*, and helps us realize
how lucky we are to make it past the age of eighteen.'

— **George Singleton**, author of *You Want More: Selected Stories*

'Steve Lambert's *Philisteens* is a coming of age novel written with humor and
grace and grit. A worthy successor to the anxious youth of Barry Hannah,
Lambert steps out all on his own as an author to note, an author to read, an
author to be remembered.'

— **Adam Van Winkle**, author of *The Red Knife Plays*

D1361987

{Philisteens}

A Novel

by
Steve Lambert

Close To The Bone
An imprint of Gritfiction Ltd

Interior Design by Craig Douglas
Cover by Steve Lambert
Front cover image credit :
"Stage Diving: don't do this at home!" By Stefan Mueller

First Printing, 2021

For our lost younger selves...

"I know I longed very much, but I didn't understand for what."
— **Saul Bellow**, *The Adventures of Augie March*

"I wanted to leave behind me a gnashing horde of bastards."
— **Barry Hannah**, *Geronimo Rex*

"Cacophony is the Florida song."
— **Al Burt**, *Becalmed in the Mullet Latitudes*

{Part One}

One

I TURNED TWELVE THE YEAR THE CHALLENGER— carrying six astronauts and Christa McAuliffe, a bright-eyed social studies teacher—exploded in a web of smoke across a perfect launch-day sky. We'd learned all about McAuliffe in the build-up to that day. The teachers of the world were proud of her. We students were proud, too, in our smart-ass way. But something went wrong.

I said, "That's not what it usually does," and looked over at Mrs. Sharpe, my home-room teacher, for an explanation. Anyone over the age of about fifteen was a sage to my mind, but Mrs. Sharpe was special; a keen intellect, *sans pareil*. She stood silent in the late morning sun, jilted, let down, grief-muted. I didn't understand what had happened beyond my dim observation of its unusualness. Like the minds of most twelve-year-olds, mine hadn't yet learned to calculate disasters. I couldn't break it up, parse it out, digest it. I glanced over at Sam, whose dad was an engineer at the

Cape, actually worked for NASA in some capacity. Sam was in G.S.P., which meant Gifted Student Program. I was in the regular classes with the rest of the rabble, and terrible at math. This horrible spectacle was, no doubt, math-related somehow. Sam said, "Neil, they're all fish food, man, all seven of 'em," which was unexpectedly adolescent and cruel and disappointing, and was not—on its face—mathematical.

When I returned home from school that day, I rushed over to mom, who sat in the bowl-shaped papasan chair folding clothes. The living room had its familiar potent smell—a mix of the sweet, fecund nose burn of cannabis and the ancient murky thickness of sandalwood. Dad was a civil-service firefighter on the air force base, but he supplemented his income as a salesman. I asked her if she'd seen what happened and she said that she had. She watched all the launches. My brusk, vermouth-breathed granddad was a retired air-force lieutenant-colonel, and had been stationed at The Cape the last five years of his service. My mother had grown up, from the age of fifteen, four blocks north of our current home, watching launches: looking up at the sky had become a habit, a mild fetish. She said that once she'd realized what happened she'd called dad at the station, but couldn't get him because he was on a run, probably due to the incident in question.

"Watched from the backyard," she said. Our house was *just barely* not on base, and only about fifteen miles from Cape Canaveral, where the Kennedy Space Center was located. My school, where Sam and I had watched, was about sixteen miles from the Cape. On most clear launch days, from our backyard or from the schoolyard, you could see the sun glint off the side of the shuttle almost all the way up. It felt special to live that close to such human pretentions. We had nothing to do with it—just passive participants—but we felt like we did. And we assumed some ownership over this tragedy. This was our collective disaster. And though this wasn't my first lesson on nature's blazing indifference, this was, I believe, my first inherent grasping that bright people with the best intentions could still fuck up and gravely injure the world and, it seems to me now, that this terrible event, external and public and witnessed by millions, was concurrent with the first whump in a string of minor detonations in my own life. This was, as it were, a beginning.

***

Sam, my crass and gifted friend, had a sister, and in my extremely limited sixth-grade way, I loved her. Hillary was a tenth grader at Apollo High School and always in some kind of trouble and, consequently, on 'restrictions' from things, like TV, or from going out on the weekends. This weekend she could watch TV, but she could not talk on the phone or go out with her friends. When I spent the night at Sam's house that Friday I was privy to some quality Hillary time.

Instead of going to my house after school, I rode my bike home with Sam. He lived only six blocks from me and my mom always felt pretty safe about my spending the night at Sam's. She also knew he was this super smart G.S.P. kid who didn't get into trouble.

Sam and I sat at the kitchen bar drinking Welch's grape soda and eating Swiss Rolls when Hillary came in from the pool, a big thick beach towel wrapped around her waist, her hair slicked back, the velvety white skin of her breasts visible at the limits of the twin triangles of her bathing suit top. She didn't even look at us. We were like phantoms. Sam made a gagging pantomime with his hands around his throat and then laughed loudly. I smiled, but couldn't keep my eyes off his sister. In response to her gangly, exceptionally bright brother's implications, Hillary let out a sarcastic, mocking laugh, whispered what sounded like 'fucktards', and walked out of the kitchen, back out to the pool. I could see her, out there, through the kitchen window. I watched her unfurl the towel and throw it onto the breeze whereupon it slowly drifted down onto the chase lounge.

"Take a picture, shithead," said Sam. He threw a wad of paper towel at me.

"Dude, give me a break. Your sister is full blown. I'm in agony." I tried to sound full blown myself, but I was a verge-of-pubescence sixth grader with no clear idea what went on between amorous humans.

"Sick bastard," said Sam. And then in a whisper, "She's a slut, you know." I thought it a bit harsh that Sam would talk about his own sister that way. It sounded especially hurtful coming from him. Even sixth graders knew, to a degree, what it meant to be a slut. A slut had too much sex. But sex itself was still mostly a mystery to me. My notions of sex consisted of nudity and vague, jumbled bedroom scenarios, nothing exactly happening, but everything imaginable happening. Applying the word slut to Hillary made her even more alluring to me. Sam mock-gagged again and finished his grape soda. Before he chucked the can into the plastic receptacle he said, "She'd traumatize you with her abilities." Yes, she would, I thought, and the agony of it all took hold of me around the waist. I felt afoul of life in some odd, immeasurable way, and stayed that way until Sam and I were well into a dark and bloody game of *Advanced Dungeons & Dragons*.

Sam and I woke up around ten the next morning and after half an hour of farting and laughing and minor cussing (mostly shits and damns and hells) we staggered out to the living room where Hillary held dominion from her station on the couch, TV remote in hand, watching MTV. She was wearing an oversized *Sex Pistols* t-shirt and black panties, which I could make out, because the shirt was worn to the point of gossamer in some spots. As I walked by I caught a gauzy glimpse of milk-colored hip. I nearly ran into a wall.

Sam's boozy mom was in the kitchen ruining bacon. We walked to the kitchen bar and sat down and watched her. She had tongs in one hand and a Virginia Slims in the other. She was, like her daughter, skimpily clad in an oversized t-shirt, hers with an iron-on of a kitten and a puppy touching noses, pink hearts floating upward from the point of contact. She took a hard drag of her cigarette and exhaled the blue smoke along with a cottony, languid "morning, boys…"

Sam's dad was not home and hadn't spent more than a few hours home at a time since the shuttle accident. All the Cape engineers had been working overtime on various projects related to finding out exactly what had caused the vehicle to explode. This, I would come to find out, was something akin to a living Hell for these men. They were working to find out, in fact, which of them was responsible, which of them would be let go, laid off, turned into a professional pariah. I couldn't imagine Sam's dad being responsible for any wrongdoing of any kind, especially a wrongdoing on the disastrous level of a shuttle explosion. Sam's dad seemed to me too smart for that. But, in truth, looking back, he was just an ordinary engineer—brilliant, for sure, but not exceptional, and the whole thing must have been an ordeal for him.

I took my plate of burnt bacon and undercooked scrambled eggs into the living room and sat in the loveseat adjacent Hillary at the couch. Being just stupid enough to hazard communication, I asked her what she was watching. It turned out she was watching, *Go Fuck Yerself*…a program with which I had no familiarity.

"It looks like *The Young Ones* to me," I said. I nipped at the edge of a piece of bacon.

"Seriously?" she slurred at me. She turned her head slowly and gave me a tired look and sighed. "Samuel! Please come retrieve your boyfriend. He's trying to do small talk with me!"

Sam's mother yelled at Hillary to be nice and Sam walked in and sat down next to me on the love seat.

"Oh my god!" said Hillary. She wrapped a ratty Strawberry Shortcake blanket, a security from her remnant childhood, around her lower body, stood up, and stormed out of the living room. The juxtaposition of the confectionary emblem of her fading childhood with the *Sex Pistols* shirt was enough to cause me momentary dysphoria.

"Mission accomplished," said Sam.

We both laughed.

"You're mom's a terrible cook, dude."

"What?!" Sam stuck a whole strip of blackish bacon in his mouth. "It's just the way I like it." I figured you had to have grown up on this shit to like it.

***

Back home, still hungry, I asked my mom to make me something to eat.

"Didn't Sam's mom make you breakfast?" She was watching TV and sewing an American-flag patch onto the sleeve of one of my dad's work shirts. My dad was still at the fire station. The shuttle incident had my dad on overtime too. They were beachcombing, my mother had told me. She would not be more specific. She didn't need to be. I could fill in the gaps. They were looking for debris from the shuttle explosion.

"Black bacon and runny eggs."

Mom made me a bowl of grits with egg and cheese mixed in just the way *I* liked it. She sat with me at the table while I ate and asked me about the sleepover. I told her that Sam's dad was working overtime too because of the shuttle explosion. My little brother, James, was out playing in the backyard, in the tree fort our dad had made with us a few years back. It wasn't the best looking tree fort, and it was somewhat rickety in places, but it was three-stories high and had secret hatches and a tire swing, and it was ours and our dad had made it with us. A few years before, a friend of mine named Ty had stayed up in the tree fort one Saturday night while I went in to eat dinner. He'd shot out a neighbors sliding glass door with my pellet rifle and tried to make a dash for it, but the neighbor, who'd watched the whole thing happen, cut him off in our side yard, and brought him to our front door.

"This here little shit shot out my door glass with a pellet gun from that goddamn tree fort in your backyard." Our neighbor, a rough, old, retired Marine originally from Tennessee, stood at our front door, holding the boy by the collar. My dad looked over at me. I shrugged.

"It was just this one here," said the neighbor. "I can tell you that much."

My dad and the neighbor called the police and Ty's parents and he never came over again.

***

After a few weeks, people seemed to set aside the shuttle disaster and things started to get back to normal. It seems odd, I thought, how quickly this happens; how happy most people are to move on. The whole thing, for me, was only beginning to sink in. I was only now feeling the weight of all that loss, and here everyone else was, getting up and walking away from it. Also, and of more immediate concern, for those three weeks of altered focus, my own personal bully,

George Nucci, had for some reason, neglected his duties. I hadn't been punched, kicked, wedgied, pushed down, insulted in front of cute girls, noogied, spat on, farted on, called belittling names, or forced to hand over my lunch money. It had been idyllic, too easy a go of things, too good to be true, but that was over now.

Sam and I sat on the bleachers in the gym at school during P.E. one Thursday. We would dress-out so that we didn't get the points deducted for participation for the day and then we'd just sit on the bleachers and talk and goof off. Our P.E. teacher, Mr. Hitchcock, seemed to be okay with that. We were in the process of contriving a weekend for ourselves. The new *Transformers* animated movie was out and Sam had convinced his mom to take us to a Friday night showing of it. I'd go home with Sam after school and spend the night. Of course, all of this was contingent on one thing, my not getting any F's on my report card. I was pretty sure I wasn't going to, but one could never be too sure about these things. I'd definitely coasted through all my classes, except for one—math. We'd been doing fractions and decimals this grading period and I was struggling with the complex nonsense of mixed numbers and improper fractions. The truth is, if I'd studied at all, I'd have been doing fine. But I wasn't. I would absorb the class lessons. I'd understand it just fine. But without studying I fairly quickly forgot the steps and was lost when it came to test time. My mind just refused to remember mathematical complexities without any reinforcement. Anyway, Friday was report card day, and Sam and I were discussing all of our tentative plans when George came walking up the bleachers toward us. Sam was about to say something, but he stopped and looked at me then looked at George. He seemed to be saying, "Well, what are you going to do?"

"What?" I said. "Go on with what you were saying."

I wasn't in the mood for any shit from George. Somehow I felt more annoyed than scared.

"Uh, okay," said Sam. "I got the new *Monster Manual* and, uh…"

By now George was standing on the bleacher bench right in front of us.

"Can I help you?" I said.

"Yeah, you can help by getting out of my fucking seat."

I looked around. Sam and I were the only people sitting on the entire bleachers.

"You can sit anywhere," I said.

George slapped Sam on the side of the head. I stood up.

"Oh, what's this!?" said George.

Sam stood up too and George pushed him back down.

"You're not going anywhere."

George took his eyes off me and looked hard and mean at Sam. I saw an opportunity and took it. While George was staring down Sam, I gave his chest a push, just a little shove to disturb his balance. It didn't take much force. He waved his arms in the air like propellers and his whole face contorted with the effort to stay planted. He fell straight back and hit his head on one of the benches of the bleachers and then rolled across the last two benches and hit the floor of the gym.

Gyms have great acoustics.

Everyone stopped what they were doing and looked our way. George's body contorted and tensed and he squealed, then he started to shake. Coach Hitchcock ran over to George and bent over him. He put his hand on George's shoulder and gently shook him. George's head lifted and he looked around. He sat up and put his head in his palm and I heard him wince. He slowly got up and looked over at me. I was still on the bleachers, in the same spot where I'd been when I'd pushed him. He didn't say anything.

I heard coach ask George what had happened. He kept looking at me, but he had a dead, oblivious look on his face. The coach asked him again, "Well, speak up. What happened?" Coach looked up at me. I shrugged and held out my arms. Finally George said, "I fell…?"

Coach called over one of George's shithead friends, a grubby guy named Pete Vogel who always wore sleeveless t-shirts, and he instructed Pete to walk George to the clinic.

I looked at Sam, who'd been totally silent the whole time.

"You believe that shit?"

"Unconscionable bastard. You better hope he doesn't ever remember what happened or he'll kick your ass. More than kick your ass. He may kill you."

This was probably true. Sam was always thinking ahead.

***

George was not at school the next day, which pleased me tremendously. But, at the end of the day, fifteen minutes before last bell, Mr. Poole handed out our report cards. The quality of the next six weeks depended on what was contained in the rectangular yellow envelope.

"All A's," said Sam with a wide brace-faced smile.

"Big surprise."

"Open yours, shithead."

I slowly peeled back the tab and pulled out the blue piece of paper. It smelled gluey, official. I felt a dim compulsion to lick the paper. I looked with one eye shut:

Art: B
P.E: C−
Language Arts: C
Science: C
Computers: C+
Math: D−

Actually, I wasn't surprised. This was a pretty standard report card for me. I'd liked to have seen a nice round D in Math, my parents were used to those by now. A D- was almost as bad as an F.

"At least it's not an F," said Sam. "You think they'll let you go?"

"The rest of my report card is pretty typical, so maybe. There aren't any real surprises here. I'd say I got an eighty-twenty chance."

***

Our weekend scheme panned out. My parents were in a decent mood Friday afternoon and only sighed and made resigned gestures upon seeing my report card. The movie was good. There were even a few cuss words in it. I spent the whole weekend at Sam's and saw his dad only once.

***

I woke up at two Saturday morning to pee and while I was negotiating my way to a not-too uncomfortable position over the toilet I heard the deadbolt on the front door turn and I heard a slight ruckus of shuffles and whispered curses. When I finished up, I walked out into the living room and saw Sam's dad. He was sprawled out across the living room couch, the most disheveled I'd ever seen a man. His mouth was wide open and his breathing was deep and scratchy. His clothes were twisted around his body, one shoe was off, and one was half on. His pants were unbuttoned, but not unzipped. He looked to me like he'd passed out about a quarter of the way through getting undressed.

I noticed something hanging out of his front jean's pocket. I tiptoed closer. It was a mangled-looking bill, hanging more than halfway out his pocket. I reached forward and silently pinched it the rest of the way out. I scurried back into the bathroom and turned the light on. Sweet Jesus! A one hundred dollar bill. This both pleased me and frightened me. I looked at it and wished it would turn into a twenty. A hundred was too much! I put it close to my eyes and examined it further, made sure I saw the one-zero-zero in the corners.

Just then I heard something. I froze. It was Sam's dad rousing.

"Uh oh," he said. And then he said, "What the… *Frances…*"

I heard the leather couch cushions squeak and wince. He was getting up. I heard footsteps. A knock on the door.

"Butter 'urry up innare, Frances!" he said.

Why did he keep saying, "Frances?" I put the money in my short's pocket and opened the door.

He looked down at me, squinting one eye, his body swaying in concentration.

"You're not one of them."

"Yes," I said, and walked around him.

He shut the door. I paused out in the hall. I could hear him hurling.

The next morning I decided not to tell Sam anything about his dad. I left relatively early, around nine, before his dad had even gotten out of bed.

The real question here, I realized, as I dug the thing out of my pocket and lay it on my bed, carefully, like a dead bird, was what in hell was a little shit like me going to do with a hundred dollars? No doubt, this was a real score. This was unprecedented. I wouldn't be able to buy anything big with it. That was for sure. Anything big would be too conspicuous. I'd have to spend it piecemeal on things that would not be noticed by my parents or close friends, meaning Sam. It kind of sucked to have that much purchasing power and not be able to take advantage of it to its fullest. Just then something else occurred to me. Where the hell was I going to break a hundred-dollar bill? A broke-ass kid with a hundred-dollar bill would be a red flag to any conscientious adult.

***

I decided that I'd be spending a good deal of this windfall at the arcade. We had this place in town called The Wizard's Den and I figured I could waste a lot of time there. I'd always wanted to but never had the occasion until now. I figured I could break the hundred there. The kids who worked there were just video-game geeks, pretty naive, so I thought it would be easy to pretend the hundred was a gift from my grandma or something and have one of them break it. One day after school I did this and it worked well enough. I got this one kid, who I somewhat knew, named Billy Nugent, to give me four twenties and four fives.

As anticipated, he said, "Where'd ya ever get a hundred bucks from?"

"Grandma," I said. "Straight A's."

"Oh," he said as he grabbed the bill and stuck in the register. "*You* got straight A's?"

I spent an hour playing games, blew ten bucks, and

then went home and ate dinner. I lay in bed that night thinking of how easy and fun it would be to spend the rest of the money now that I'd got the bill broke. I could blow a lot of it at The Den, but there were other places too. There was food. I could buy all kinds of crap that I normally was not able to or that my mom wouldn't let me buy. I thought maybe I'd buy a fishing pole and tackle one day and go fishing and then just ditch it all or give it away once I was done. I'd been wanting to work on my fishing proficiency. There were endless possibilities, I thought, as my eyelids slowly descended, and my thoughts began to swirl and morph into the strange but familiar spectacle of dreams.

Two

A S SIXTH GRADERS WE WERE THE OLDEST kids on campus. We thought we were badass and, except for George Nucci, I had no worries. My little brother, James, was only three-years-old so I'd never have to worry about suffering the indignity of sharing a school with him. It was now early April and we began to realize that we only had two more months of school until summer break—and after summer break, seventh grade, junior high school.

"We'll go back to being shit-birds again," said Sam one Saturday in the middle of a perfectly good game of King's Quest on his Tandy 1000.

"Don't think about it," I said. "That's a long ways away."

"No it isn't, man. Five months. Five months and we will be walking the halls in a completely different school with bastards with beards. You think Nucci's bad? There will be dudes with beards who can drive giving you swirlies."

I didn't know what a swirly was, but it didn't sound that bad, which was a pretty good indication that it was probably unbearable. I was about to ask him to tell me all he knew about swirlies when the door slammed. It was middle of the day on a Saturday. We heard some grumbling and a commotion and then something breaking against the floor. I got out of my chair and Sam put his hand on my chest and told me to stay—he'd go check. As soon as he left the room I ran to the bedroom door and put my ear to it. I heard Sam and then I heard his dad. Sam was talking quietly and his dad was talking loudly, but he sounded bad, the way he had the night I took the money. After a few minutes I didn't hear anything so I tiptoed back to the computer and sat down and waited. I waited for about twenty minutes. I walked cautiously out of Sam's bedroom and walked into the living room and looked around. No one. No sounds. Sam's parents' bedroom door was closed. I stood there deciding what to do. It was probably time to leave. I was about to turn and go back to Sam's room and get my shoes when Hillary walked in through the front door.

When she saw me she stopped. She put her house keys in her purse and zipped her purse, the whole time staring at me. She began walking toward me. She was chewing neon green gum and I wanted to be that gum. I wanted to taste her saliva. I wanted to put my tongue in her mouth and flit it around. She got about two feet from me and stood there chewing her gum at me, staring, saying nothing. I just stood there, too, waiting—for what, I didn't know, but I didn't care either. Anything good, I thought, would happen here, even if it was something bad. With Hillary I took what I could get. She could have beat and battered me and that would have been okay. She just stared and chewed. "You break the lamp?" she said. "No," I said.

"I think your dad did." She looked past me and then back at me. At a loss, I smiled. She puckered her lips and I thought, Jesus! And I leaned forward and closed my eyes and Hillary hawked her neon gum, coated in her saliva, at my face. It splatted into my closed eye and fell to the floor. I could smell it, her saliva, like cigarettes and gum, and maybe beer, and I opened my eyes and she was smirking at me. I still smiled, even wider now, and I took my hand and wiped my eye and then licked my hand. Her smirk went to a grimace of disgust. I bent over and picked up the wad of gum and held it and looked Hillary in the eye. "Oh, God!" she said. "You wouldn't." And I did, and it was wonderful—warm and moist and Hillary-flavored.

Right then Sam came out of his parents' room and saw Hillary and me facing each other.

"What are you two doing?" he said. He looked upset. He looked like maybe he'd been crying, or like he was going to.

"Nothing," I said. "I better be heading home."

He nodded. Hillary looked me over and shook her head and walked past me.

I chewed that piece of gum for hours. I chewed it until it was dry as a piece of rubber. I imagined that I sucked every bit of Hillary-ness out of it and then I spit it into my hand and smelled of it. I didn't want to throw it away so I mashed it into the back left corner of my t-shirt drawer.

***

After watching my mom prep dinner for an hour, I walked to the Wizard's Den and spent about an hour playing *Galaga* and watching Fitz, this video-game genius kid, play *Super Mario Bros.* He knew every nook and cranny of that game. It was amazing. I wondered vaguely if I'd ever be that good at something. I figured I was probably too lazy for that level of proficiency. I ate too many cherry Twizzlers and got a rumbling stomach-ache and went home. I lay in bed and watched Tom & Jerry on my black and white TV. By the time Tom & Jerry was over I felt a little better. I got out of bed and went to my dresser and got out Hillary's gum. It was dry and hard and faded, not so neon now. I sniffed it and it had no scent at all. I stuck my tongue to it. I walked back to the bed with it and lay down and put the gum in my mouth and kept it there while I took the money out of the pencil box in my bedside table drawer. I counted it. I had sixty-nine dollars and some change left. Tomorrow was Sunday and I felt like it would be nice to go fishing. I put the money away and lay and thought about things: Hillary's lips, and how amazing they must be to touch; the flesh of the parts of her I'd never seen, would never see, like her breasts, which I imagined felt like velvet. I wondered what her nipples looked like. I thought about putting my mouth around them. I thought about the impossibility of it and how I'd probably be too scared to do it, to do anything, were I presented with the possibility. I thought about Fitz, the *Mario Bros.* genius; how did he get that way? How did anyone get that good at something? Could I ever be that good at something? Did I have it—whatever *it* was—in me to be good at something? I thought about how my dad was always at work and when he was home he was usually too tired to do anything, like play catch or go fishing, with me or James. I thought and chewed at the softening piece of gum. It tasted like nothing. My thoughts tasted like nothing. I took the gum out and looked at it. It looked better. It had been revived somewhat, but it had lost all traces of Hillary. I put it back in my mouth and swallowed it. It was the last thing to do with it. I couldn't have thrown it away.

***

The night that Sam's dad had come home drunk he'd found out that he would be laid off from his shuttle engineer job. Sam's mom did not work so they were in a bad situation. At school on Monday, at lunch, Sam had told me about this.

"He's not the only one. Lots of engineers are being let go—not fired, but laid off."

"What's gonna happen? Are you guys gonna have to move or something?"

"Maybe. I don't know. My parents don't talk about it a lot and I don't ask them."

I didn't know what to say, but I went for positive reinforcement. That's what you do, I figured. You said positive things, even if you didn't believe them.

"He'll find something," I said.

Sam nodded and poked at his meatloaf.

"Hillary's out of control. She's been skipping school and sneaking out and stuff like that. She has this boyfriend named Huff, whatever that means, and he drives one of those shitty Volkswagen buses and surfs and crap."

I didn't want to hear about this, I didn't want to hear about Hillary's extracurricular activities. I didn't want to have my vague, intimate imaginings invaded by lunkheaded surfer dudes.

"Hey, man. Geoffrey Lewis is selling his comic book collection. Let's go by his place sometime this week and see what he has." I didn't really care, but I needed to change the subject. We made plans to go to Geoff's on Wednesday after school.

***

Later that day, something occurred to me. George Nucci had

disappeared. My own personal bully was gone. I hadn't seen him in school for at least a week. I was glad for that, but I was curious about what had happened. Nobody seemed to know. I asked around and got nothing but shrugs and *who cares* and *fuck offs*. But on Wednesday, walking home from Geoff's house with an arm load of *Classic X-Men*, I ran into Chris Buckley on his skateboard. We were not friends. He was an eighth-grader who was friends with Benny Nucci, George's older brother, and he was one of the nicer guys in that crew. He'd actually talk to you, instead of punching you or pushing you down.

"Hey Chris," I said.

He stopped and flipped his skateboard up into the air and grabbed it.

"What's up, dweeb." He acted like he was going to hit me. "You flinched."

"That's a sweet skateboard. I've been thinking of starting skating."

"Might get rid of some of that baby fat."

Baby fat? Did I have baby fat? "Do you know why George Nucci hasn't been at school?"

"You didn't hear about that?"

I shrugged.

"Got hit by a car."

"Musta been bad."

"Yeah." He hoisted his skateboard and wiggled the back truck. He stopped and pulled a small tool out of a sack he wore on his waist and put the board down on the ground, upside down, and went to tightening a bolt. "Actually, he wasn't *hit*. He was, more like, run over. He won't be back to school at all, not till next year." He flipped his board over and got on it, gave it a push and shimmied back and forth, checking his tightening job.

"That's crazy."

"Yep." He gave it another push and waved. "Later, shit-stick."

***

By Friday something else was beginning to occur to me. I stole money from a man who was now unemployed. Sam's dad needed the money a lot more than I did. I didn't actually *need* money. A sick feeling crept through me and I was preoccupied with thoughts of Sam's dad, drunk and fumbling about in his living room, wondering where he'd mislaid his money. But the truth was, he probably didn't even know. He'd been so drunk, he may have thought he spent it all or lost it, but being twelve, I didn't know anything about that. I'd never been drunk. I didn't really know what happened to a person when they were drunk. But I did know guilt. I felt so guilty in fact that when Sam called up and asked me to spend the night, I said no. I made up an excuse, said I was not feeling well, which was somewhat true, and I stayed home. He seemed really bummed out, which made me feel even worse. He'd really wanted me to spend the night. There was something like loneliness in his voice, and desperation—he did not want to be alone in his sad house, with only his family. Had I not stolen the money, I'd have jumped at the invitation to spend the night.

Making matters worse, my parents soon after informed me that they were going out and that if I was staying home, I'd be staying home with not only James, but the babysitter they'd already arranged for. I couldn't call Sam back and say, "Hey, man. I am miraculously better. I'll spend the night." I was stuck—a selfish dick who was going to spend the evening with his little-shit brother and a babysitter.

The babysitter, a pretty sixteen-year-old girl named Heather Trenton, was not bad, as babysitters go, but the thought of being home with James and a baby-sitter was repellent. The very word babysitter was repellent. In my mind, I was beyond being babysat. In fact, I was growing accustomed to being the babysitter myself. If my parents were going out for only an hour or two, they would leave James with me. But this time, they said, they would be gone until after midnight.

***

Heather put James to bed at nine-thirty and then came back out into the living room and sat on the couch. I was lying on the floor watching TV.

"You're next, mister," she said.

"Can I just finish watching this?" *The Creature from the Black Lagoon* was on and I hadn't seen it in a while. "There's only about fifteen minutes left." I had no idea how much of the movie was left, but fifteen minutes seemed believable.

She let me finish and then she walked me into my room and watched me climb into bed. She stood next to the light switch and smiled at me. It seemed weird. She was pretty though. She lived on our street, a few houses down, so I'd grown up seeing her often. She was tall and athletic. She played tennis for Apollo High and she wore tight sporty clothes all the time, very short shorts, and you could see the shape of her body. I lay there, staring, not speaking.

She walked across the room and sat down on the bed. She put her hand on my foot. She had a thoughtful expression on her face. What is happening? I thought. But, still, I didn't speak. I started to sweat. Within seconds my legs were practically dripping with sweat. She just sat there staring at me, smiling.

"Can I ask you something?" she said finally.

I just nodded.

"Do you think I'm pretty?"

I shrugged.

She smirked and breathed out a quick laugh.

"I guess," I said.

"Oh, you guess?"

I nodded. My body felt like it was vibrating.

"Have you ever kissed a girl?"

I shrugged, again.

"You either have or you haven't," she said.

"No. Not really. No, I haven't."

She leaned over and kissed me on the lips and I could smell her, like an exotic-flower—clean and fragrant and other things. My lips tingled. I didn't even pucker up. I let her lips do all the kissing. I was a passive participant. She moved back and looked at me, smirk back on her face.

"How was that?" she said.

By now I was barely capable of any kind of lucid thinking or talking. Barely capable of movement. Dumb with terror and excitement. I had no idea what was happening. I was experiencing some kind of paralysis.

"Have you ever seen a woman's breasts before?"

This outrageous question elicited no response from me, except for a further moving into myself, a stress-related withdrawal, then, when I could move no further inward, I moved slowly out of myself and there was a thrumming. I was a husk.

She stood up and pulled off her shirt and when she did her breasts hoisted upward just slightly and dropped, for a moment, overfilling the cups of her bra. They were large and brown and terrifying. That is, seeing them terrified me— and aroused me.

It was too much, though, and so unexpected, that the terror and surprise were beginning to take over. I went nuts on the inside, as if my interior was convulsing, but my body didn't budge.

She sat down again and reached back and undid her bra, and off it came, her breasts heaving down and surging into their fullness. She was beaming around the eyes, hadn't, it seemed, the slightest feeling of uneasiness about what she was doing. She looked down at them and then looked at me, an eyebrow raised, as if to say, Does this meet with your approval? She took my hand and put the palm of it on her right breast, right over the nipple, and I, lost in some zone of perception in which I'd never before operated, did nothing. I was there and not there. I could feel her nipple, hardened, and I could feel the impossible roundness of her delicate breast and I couldn't believe what was happening to me. I realized my eyes were closed now and I was picturing all of this instead of actually seeing it. I opened my left eye and saw that Heather's eyes were closed, thank goodness, and her head was thrown back. She began moving my hand around, softly, on her breast and then she pressed my hand into it, warm and tender and real.

Finally she opened her eyes and smiled at me and when she did I closed my eyes again. She withdrew my hand and put it back exactly where she'd found it. We both sat there for a moment. I opened my eyes and looked at her, and she watched me look at her. This was some kind of thing for her. She got a kick out of all this. Finally she put her bra back on, then her shirt. She stood up and looked down at me and blew me a kiss.

"Good night," she said.

Shrugging was all I had anymore, my sole note of communication.

She turned off the light and walked out, and I lay there for some time, motionless, replaying the experience, over and over, until I drifted to sleep, wherein I dreamt of the experience, over and over, until I woke at hearing the commotion of my parents returning very late. I heard them thanking Heather, and I heard Heather's cheerful, tennis-court voice say, no problem, it was my pleasure, and the boys were great, and any time. She left, and I lay there, still, and disbelieving.

To this day a part of me is still there, in disbelief, wondering if it all really happened.

Three

MONDAY, AT SCHOOL, I COULDN'T WAIT TO tell Sam about what had happened with Heather, the sitter. The sitter! She'd sat right down on the side of my bed and showed me a glimpse of something. I felt more advanced now. Bolder. I'd kissed a girl, touched a breast, and my bully was bedridden till next school year. I felt more independent, like a pioneer. I was ready to pan for gold or something. Emboldened, I felt ready for anything. (Never mind that the experience, in the moment, had been crippling.)

Sam didn't look so good, at lunch, when I finally got a chance to talk to him. I saw him sitting at our table and walked up and sat down next to him.

"I've got something to tell you, man," I said, "and you're not gonna believe it."

"I've got something to tell you, too. You can go first, though."

"What's wrong? Everything okay?"

"Yeah, everything's fine. What do you want to tell me?"

"I'm not even sure how to start. Do you know who Heather Trenton is?"

"Yeah, a little. She used to be friends with my sister, in the ninth grade. But they kind of went different ways or something. She's kind of a jock girl. Hillary's... not that."

"Well, she babysat my brother the other night." I wasn't about to say she babysat both of us. "And she came into my room and kissed me, right on the lips, and let me touch her boob."

"What?"

Admittedly, I'd butchered the account of it. I wasn't much of a storyteller. In hindsight, I should have lead with *I touched a boob*. That should have been my hook, then I could have recounted the evening in greater detail.

"Yes. She let me touch her boob."

"Did you ask her if you could touch it or something?"

"No. It's hard to explain. She came into my room and sat on my bed—"

"Wait! She tucked you in? You got tucked in by a babysitter, basically."

Smart little shit...

"Sure, think of it that way, if you want. But, I got to touch a boob. I think that's the heart of the matter here. Have you touched a boob? Other than your mom's?"

"Were they big? She has big ones, doesn't she?"

"Oh, yeah. They were big. They were... immense."

We laughed. Sam put his hands in his shirt and made like he had boobs and made smoochie-kissy faces at me, and we laughed some more.

"Wait," he said. He suddenly looked serious. "The

fact is: you were sexually abused. That's sexual abuse. She *sexually* abused you."

I hadn't thought of that, those words. I had nothing to say.

"Are you okay? Do you need to talk to somebody?"

We both sat listening to the din of cafeteria chaos around us.

"Dude," said Sam. "I'm kidding." Then he got solemn and took up his fork and pushed his spaghetti around. "We're moving," he mumbled.

"What?!"

"Yeah, my dad has lined up a job at some other company, Northrop-Grumman. They build airplanes and junk."

"When?"

"They're gonna let me finish out the school year since it's practically over anyway."

We decided right there that we'd have to do some serious hanging out for the rest of the school year. As much as possible. Serious, epic, insane hanging out. Record breaking stuff. Sam even suggested our getting into a little trouble. "I've never really gotten into any trouble. I'd like to get a feel for it before junior high. Seems like the right thing to do. Seems preparatory somehow."

"Kind of like touching a grown woman's boob?"

He brightened up and made some more smoochy faces and did a hubba-hubba thing with his hands in his shirt.

***

Everything was pretty standard, hanging out wise, until late May. I spent the night at Sam's house a lot and we stayed up late playing video games and eating garbage and swimming in his pool. But the sense that time was running out for us began to foster in us a sense of desperation. In the last weekend of May, while everyone was out of Sam's house, we conspired to do something ground-breaking, something all new and slightly dangerous.

"My parents have a liquor cabinet," said Sam. "In their room. It's locked up, because they don't trust Hillary, but I know where the key is. My mom has hidden it in front of me, because she trusts me."

We got the key, which was in a drawer next to their bed, which had an unsettlingly adult smell emanating from it, sweet and sick, and we went over to the cabinet and unlocked it and opened it up. Our eyes were met with the sinful glint and gleam of the bottles, one after another, varying in height, bringing to mind a city's skyline at night. Sam grabbed one and held it up and jostled the brown liquid and took the cap off and smelled of it and made a face and said, "Not that one," re-capped it and put it back. He picked up one that was a deep candy-green and it said melon ball on the label and it smelled better so we gave it a try. It wasn't too bad. But we decided we couldn't drink a lot of it.

I picked the next one. Gin. I'd heard of it and liked the sound of it. It smelled bad, but not as bad as the brown one had smelled, so I took a good gulp of it and my throat felt like a pinewood fire was in it. I almost puked and Sam laughed and he got up off the floor and walked to his mom's dresser and opened a drawer and pulled out a pack of cigarettes.

"Yes," I said. "Perfect…"

We ended up settling on red wine, a Merlot, and there we sat, smoking Virginia Slims and drinking wine, getting drunk, whatever that meant, and feeling like we'd never felt before. I felt almost adult. I'd kissed a girl, goddamnit, and touched a boob and was now breaking the law, drinking alcohol and smoking cigarettes. We'd broke out and into an adult world. We didn't even do that much talking. We were experiencing too many things for the first time to be talking. Our eyes were wide and we had huge smiles on our faces and we were slow-moving and intent and entranced, mesmerized… drunk. But it did all come to a momentary full-stop when I looked over at Sam and saw him looking up and over me, with an *oh-shit* look on his face. I turned around and there she stood, smirking, standing in the doorway.

"You guys are fucked," she said, quite pleased with the prospect.

I looked at Sam and he looked at me and we both busted out laughing. Things were different.

"Whatever, *sis*," said Sam, and he took a long manly drag of the skinny cigarette and blew it out with a fit of coughs.

Now she laughed. She walked in and sat down and grabbed the bottle of wine and took a delinquent swig. She put it down and took the pack of cigarettes off the floor and lit one. We watched. An expert was at work. She took hard, experienced pulls on the cigarette and exhaled dense clouds of fully-savored smoke. We were being outclassed.

"That's how you do that," she said.

I gave it a try and my throat got gritty and hot, and my head felt light and I felt like puking, but I didn't want to let on with Hillary sitting there.

"That's a little better," she said. *Better.* Jesus! Quasi-approval from a beautiful woman.

It might be because I was drunk, but Hillary looked particularly lovely to me. She wore tight jeans and Chucks and a too-small, worn out *Minor Threat* t-shirt, with a little black sheep on it. Her hair had recently been cut, too, into a bob, and it was dyed pitch black, which made her skin look even paler.

"I don't know if you've heard," I said, "But I've recently had a sexual encounter." I attempted another drag of my cigarette.

Sam sputtered with sarcasm and smeared out his cigarette in the ashtray.

"He touched the babysitters boob!" he said.

"She wasn't my babysitter. She was my brother's."

"Heather Trenton! She kissed him nighty-night!" he sputtered some more.

"Heather Trenton?" she said. "I know her."

"Yeah," I said in a dismissive tone. "She's not bad."

"Actually," said Hillary, "she's gorgeous." She looked down dejectedly when she said it.

"Hang on!" I said. "Just hang on a damn second here!" I couldn't take seeing my girl this way, all down on herself. "Hillary..." But I stopped there.

She looked at me with a half-smile on her face. Swigged the wine.

"What? Spit it out." She actually wanted to hear what I had to say.

"Yeah, spit it out Boob Man," said Sam.

"She is gorgeous, Heather Trenton. And her boob was... quintessential..."

Sam laughed at the inappropriateness of the word. We all laughed.

"But you..." I continued. "Hillary, you are..." I took up the gin and hit it hard. "You are just...exquisite...to me."

"Holy fudging shit!" said Sam. "This is a toxic environment..." He stood up and walked out and left us there sitting on the floor. I couldn't believe it either. I'd spoken a hard libidinous truth for the first time in my pathetic little life.

Hillary put the bottle down and started crawling toward me. I leaned back. She got face to face with me and stopped.

"You're just a maggoty little shit," she whispered. She moved closer and as she did I moved back and it got to where she was hovering over me, and I was lying down on the floor, looking into her eyes, and she did it. She kissed me on the lips. Everything else, in that moment, was nothing, non-existent. I felt as small as the end of a sharpened pencil lead. There was tiny, microscopic me and a warm hum, which was Hillary, all around me. I was engulfed. This was heaven. I told myself that: *You're in heaven, man.*

After a while I opened my eyes and she was still there, hovering, humming, reverberating. She sat down on me, right on my lap, and she did almost the same eyebrow thing that Heather had done, the one that said, *Are you getting all this? Do you realize what's happening here?* Then she took my hand, just like heather had done, and she slid it under her *Minor Threat* t-shirt, right under the sheep, and stuck it under the cup of her bra and pressed my hand into her left breast. She let go.

She smirked down at me. I closed my eyes again.

"What do you think?" she said. "I've got nothing on Heather, huh?"

Too busy thinking to myself, *you are the luckiest maggoty shit alive* to answer, I just lay there. I gave it a slight squeeze. Her breast felt different than Heather's had. It was softer and her nipple was different, but it was just as amazing, in its own way.

"I asked you a question?" she said. "What do you think?"

"Well," I said, finally. "It *is* smaller."

This was the wrong thing to have said. She smacked me across the face and got up and stood there glaring at me.

"That's not what I meant! It's only the second one I've ever felt in my whole stupid life. It was—"

She took the heel of her foot and stabbed it into my crotch and then turned to walk away and ran right into her dad, standing quietly at the threshold.

I jumped up. Hillary stood behind her dad and behind her was Sam. Sam's mom didn't seem to be anywhere around.

I walked, head down, out into the living room and stood next to Sam.

"You," he said, pointing at Hillary, "go to your room."

She cocked a hip out and took a few steps forward.

"Fine," she said. She turned, though, and walked up to me. Got so close our bodies were almost touching. "A word of advice," she said, "notice when you are lucky, and act accordingly."

"To your room!" their dad repeated.

She turned around flicked her dad off and walked into her room.

Jesus, I thought. How will I ever like another girl?

"As for you two..." he said. "Sam, to your room. You, go home. And I don't want to see you again. Understand?"

"Yes sir," I said, gave him a salute. "I understand. I read you loud and clear." I turned and waved to Sam. "See you around," I said.

"See you around," he said, smiling. He made a smooch face at me and his dad smacked him across the top of his head.

I headed home, slightly drunk, in the hot late spring day, and felt good, despite what had happened. Despite what Sam's dad had said. In fact, I was really kind of strutting. I realized I had some money in my pocket, some of Sam's dad's money, and I stopped and pulled it out and looked at it. I stood there and contemplated my actions leading to this moment. I'd made some poor decisions, admittedly, up to now. I thought about Christa McAuliffe, Mrs. Sharpe's plain but pretty teacher-hero who was gone forever, and I thought about my dad, imagined him out there beachcombing, looking for pieces of our collective tragedy, pieces of our *conquistadores' craft.* I thought about the other six astronauts whose lives' were lost that day, and I thought about Sam's situation. It was unfortunate, too, but not the sort of thing one spent too much time on… But when there was a Hillary involved, whom I would most likely never see again… But I was okay with that, because she'd given of herself, in a way, and I felt like I could move on… I could go further, with some degree of confidence, thanks to Hillary. And thanks to Heather, too, I supposed. As traumatic as it had been, it had been glorious, too. And there was the fact that for the foreseeable future I had no bully to worry about. Here I was, twelve-years-old, and I'd done some things. I'd had some experiences. I'd macheted my own way through the thickets. Yes, despite it all, things were good. I put the money, *my* money, damnit, back into my pocket and turned around, walked back by Sam's house, the doors and windows closed, looking dark inside, looking sober and resigned inside. I headed to the Wizard's Den, where I'd blow a shitload of money on video games and candy and soda, and maybe, if I continued to be lucky, there'd be something more on the other side of it all, something completely unpredictable.

Four

AS SOON AS THE SCHOOL YEAR HAD ENDED, Sam and his family moved. His parents had been ready for a month, practically revving the engine of the loaded car and waiting for the last day of school so that they could peel off the driveway and out of town. We said goodbye, unceremoniously, on the Sunday before they left. They'd be leaving the next day and his dad had cooled off enough to let him come by our place for an hour so we could wrap things up. It was depressing and we didn't really talk that much. We laughed a little, recounting our last day together. I told him I was worried about Hillary. "She's gonna miss me, man. It'll definitely be hard on her to be away from me." He called me an idiot. He said he'd call me once they got a phone at the new place and he left. And that was it. End of story.

***

In the beginning, without Sam, the summer felt long, which under normal circumstances would have been a good thing. But, as it was, I found myself bored and actually looking forward to the next school year. It was going to be different, anyway. I wasn't going back to elementary school. I would be going to junior high. Part of me was scared, but I was also looking forward to it.

About three weeks into summer, though, I met Coleman Whitcomb Jackson III, C.J. He wasn't new in town, but somehow I'd never met him.

I was walking home after an early afternoon of farting around at the beach. I think it was a Sunday, but I'm not sure. During the summertime in central Florida, every day, it seems, is the same day. It's like three months of freakishly hot Fridays. The only thing, for me, that ever stood out about a Florida summer is the afternoon storms. Apocalyptic tempests lasting only a few minutes. They're the best thing about our summers. Other than that, you kind of lose track, and something about the beach and its unrelenting sameness compounds this.

He was walking in the opposite direction, holding a skateboard under his arm. As we got close to each other, he put up his hand, like he had a question for the teacher. "Hey, man. You live around here?"

"Uh, yeah," I said.

He pointed at his skateboard.

"I need some tools. A screwdriver and some pliers, at least. My trucks are loose."

I was pretty sure we had those things, so I told him to follow me.

I took him into our messy garage and he did whatever he had to do to his skateboard. He stood on it and rocked back and forth.

"That'll work till I can get back home."

"I've always wanted to do that," I said.

"What? Skateboard?"

"Yeah. Is it hard?"

"Nah—yeah, at first, maybe. But you pick it up pretty quick, I guess." He got off of it and pointed at it. "Go ahead, give it a try."

I stood on the thing and rocked it back and forth like he'd done. Seemed okay.

"I have an old board at home you could use—to get started on. You can have it. It's not a Nash or anything. It's good enough to learn on."

I didn't know what a 'Nash' was, but I assumed it was a low-quality skateboard. Hell it didn't matter to me either way. I took him up on his offer and got on my bike and rode home with him. This time of year it didn't get dark until nearly nine, so I had time. He pulled the beat-up old thing out from under his bed and handed it to me. It wasn't so bad, had a scuffed-up graphic of a pumpkin-headed scarecrow on the bottom of it, and the name Jeff Kendall in pink just below it. We hung out in his room for a while, listened to music, some band called *The Misfits*, who kind of freaked me out at first, but the more I listened to them the more I liked them. And as I was leaving, with my new old skateboard in hand, his sister, Natalie, emerged from the shower, towel wrapped around her trim, brown body. She had very short pink hair and a small, cute face. She stopped and stared at me for a second, smiled, and walked off. I felt on the edge of something.

***

C.J. was pretty good at skateboarding and he tried teaching me the basics of it, but I was a hard study. It would take me a solid year before I'd learn the most important thing of all, the thing that was the bedrock of practically all street skateboarding, the Ollie, which is essentially jumping up in the air, while bringing the board up with you, and landing back down on top of the board, while rolling along. After that, things came more quickly. But until then, C.J. was patient with me and, most importantly, didn't make me feel like a poser while I was learning. In a way, he was more grown up about things like that than I was—then again, most kids our age were.

CJ had an athletic grace about him. He was tall and wiry, and girls liked him, but he didn't seem to notice or care. He was only going into the sixth grade and he already had facial hair. Physical things, like skateboarding, came naturally to him. Hell, I was a grade ahead of him and had fewer friends, less respect, and no opposite-sex experience to speak of, unless you counted the wonderful trespasses Hillary and Heather had allowed me. No prospects, either. But I muddled along, and C.J. let me, which was the main thing. I had someone cool, in the true essence of the word, to school me up, patiently, and for me to be seen around, even if he was younger than I was. This situation would prove to be a strain on my only other steady pal.

***

Geoff and I had always been friends, but in Sam's absence, early on, he fairly quickly stepped in. Geoff was a gawky rising seventh grader, into comics and video games and reading fantasy novels—sword and sorcery stuff. I'd met him at The Wizard's Den when we were in the fifth grade. He, Sam and I had become pretty good friends. We'd have sleepovers at his place and debate things like who the hottest female Marvel superhero was. His favorite was Storm, from

The *X-Men* and mine was Jean Grey, also from The *X-Men*.

But that didn't last very long because once C.J. and I started hanging, everything changed. The change was subtle at first, but it ramped up substantially after the start of the school year.

It became clear to me, once I had properly acclimated to junior high, that there were groups. I know them now as cliques, but at the time, I just saw that people had kind of accreted into groups. Nerds, punks, surfers, jocks, preps, metalheads, new-wave chicks (and one gay new-wave dude), skinheads, skaters. (This hadn't really happened in elementary school. There were just people you liked and people you didn't, or people who liked you and people who didn't). Some of these groups overlapped, on certain occasions, like at lunch. If your group was lacking in members at a given time, it was an unspoken thing that there were certain other groups you could pull proxy group members from. All of this is familiar to anyone who went to an American junior high school, but, then, as I was experiencing it for the first time, it was a real awakening. Completely new.

So I had to group-up, and my friendship to Geoff fell victim to that necessity. He went with the nerds and I went with the skate-rats. It made sense at the time. When you're twelve or thirteen, you feel the gravitational pull of your people and you go. I often consider what my life's trajectory would have been had I not met CJ. Would I have joined the nerd group? Who would I be now? Would my life have been substantially different? Perhaps.

For now, it was still summertime and none of that had happened yet and I was still walking the line between the two friendships and enjoying both and doing the best I could to fill the void of Sam's absence. I wanted for something gritty and real to happen before school started up again, something akin to my last day at Sam's, but more in-depth.

Heather and Hillary had given me a glimpse and I wanted more, which was another reason why I leaned a little more toward CJ than I did Geoff. They both had older sisters, but CJ's sister was more to my liking, and in the Venn diagram of my sad little life her group overlapped a little with mine, being that I was a fledgling skater dude and she was an older punk girl. It seemed, at the time, to make sense.

That summer had things funky at home too, but the full extent to which they had grown to would not be apparent to me for some time. Suffice it to say, that that summer I began to notice a tension, like a dense fog, descend on our little abode, that did not lift for some time, and only under drastic but welcome circumstances. My dad barely spoke and, when home from work, slept a lot during the day, and my mom spent a lot of time sitting in the bay window in our front room. It had become her perch. She sat and had her morning coffee there. She read magazines there. She folded laundry there. She talked on the phone there. Always there. Always sitting there, anxious, and periodically glancing up and down the road, like a teenaged girl waiting for her date to arrive.

***

At first, things plodded along, me and C.J. skateboarding around town, him showing me tricks and me, mostly, failing miserably, but doggedly determined. On other days I'd be at Geoff's place, reading *X-Men,* and swimming in his pool. An uneventful, humdrum, slow and hot summer, just fine, until these two worlds merged and exploded, like when you drip water into a pan of hot oil.

It should be pointed out that I did not hit what they call a growth spurt until the eighth grade. In the seventh grade I was short and pudgy, about five-foot-three and round. Both Geoff and CJ, in the throes of pubescence, were taller than me, and pimply and hairy and gangly and wiry and given to tempers. My prepubescent, hairless state had me innocent of those *tempers*. I was still blissfully boyish and naïve to flaring, out-of-nowhere anger, and when I was confronted with it for the first time, it completely baffled me.

CJ and I were skating down a neighborhood road that intersected with Geoff's, on our way to this church parking lot where there were launch ramps and quarter pipes and fun-boxes set up. We were about halfway there when I saw Geoff walking up ahead. He was wearing nothing but cut-off blue jeans—no shirt or shoes. His body was bent forward just a bit and he almost walked right by us without noticing.

I jumped off my board and popped it up into my hand.

"Geoff," I said, and his head moved slowly up to me and his eyes looked glazed over.

"Oh… hey."

CJ was standing next to me, almost a foot taller, almost exactly the size of Geoff, only CJ was less skinny and more wiry and in contrast to pale Geoff, looked much darker. It was, in fact, in contrast to Geoff, in this moment, that I for the first time thought of CJ as *black*. It was the first time the word ever seemed even remotely applicable to him. CJ was *black*. Geoff was *white*. I was white. I remember, at odd moments after this, looking at myself—black hair, brown eyes, tan skin—and thinking that the words—black, white—seemed completely inadequate and not at all descriptive of how anyone actually looked. Could I really call myself *white*? Could you really call anyone *white*? Could you really call anyone *black*? These were lazy applications. But still, as inappropriate as the two words were to the description of the boys themselves, there was something about the moment, as it happened, that brought the words to mind. And in that moment, strangely, the words assumed, if not a rightness, a certain applicability that made me feel uncomfortable, and makes me uncomfortable now.

"What's up, man?" I touched his shoulder, which was sweaty, almost slimy.

He lifted his shoulders and looked around, and then made to scratch his shoulder where I'd pushed him. "I don't know. Just walking."

At that point I realized that CJ and Geoff had never met. They knew of each other, from school and from my talking to each about the other, but they'd never met.

"Geoff," I said, "this is CJ."

They both nodded, without a word.

"We're headed to the church." 'The church' needed no explanation, everyone who lived in the area, even non-skaters, knew about it.

"All right," said Geoff. "Have fun skating." He started to walk off, head back down, slightly bent at the waist, as if he'd gotten too tall for his center of gravity.

"Have *fun*?" said CJ.

Geoff stopped and turned and looked at CJ and then at me.

"Yeah, whatever. Have fun." Geoff's brow was tensed up and he looked ticked off. "On your little skateboards."

CJ walked a little closer to Geoff, board tucked under his arm. He got about three feet away. "Put a fucking shirt on, man! Who walks around like that?"

Geoff's eyes got wide and he got up on his toes. "I do, dude."

I wasn't sure what was happening, but I was at once entranced and repelled. I'd never in my life felt like behaving this way, this aggressively. But something in these two boys had been turned on and they seemed to me to almost be enjoying it. This was teenager shit, for sure, and I just wasn't there yet.

"You're not allowed to say *dude*, dude. You're too much of a kook to use that word—with your tight-ass jeans and bird-chest."

Geoff put an arm out, almost zombielike, to push CJ, and CJ batted his arm away and threw down his skateboard and had Geoff in a head-lock and they were fighting, just like that. I had no idea what to do. I'd never seen either of them behave this way. I wanted to stop it, but I wanted to let them go for it, to watch and see what happened.

Neither of them were talking, just tussling and grunting, and eventually CJ got Geoff down on the ground, his head stuck under his arm, and I got a look at Geoff's face, it was strained and his eyes were closed. It seemed like maybe he couldn't breathe and I was about to jump in there and break them up and Geoff sort of slid out and bounded to his feet, his eyes still closed. CJ got up and came at him, his eyes wide and crazy, and Geoff put his arm out and just said, "Stop. I don't want to fight with you." And then he opened his eyes.

CJ looked confused and he glanced at me, maybe to gage my reaction. I just shrugged and frowned, as if to say, "Dude, I don't know." Besides I was in awe of both of them at this point.

CJ picked up his skateboard.

Geoff watched him, and it was like I wasn't there again, to either of them. I was like a phantom, but this time it was just me.

"See you later, man," I said to Geoff, and he nodded, without looking at me, and CJ and I turned and walked towards the church, quietly, neither of us saying a word. I'd located a new space of adolescence. I had only been a spectator, but I'd been there with them, had watched it go down. We said nothing as we walked and I thought about it for a while. Finally I realized the small absurdity of the fact that we were walking while carrying a means of transportation. I threw down my skateboard, jumped on it and gave it several hard pushes. It felt good, so I kicked more, until I was furiously pushing the skateboard along, as fast as I could, then I was yelling something, releasing something inside me, something that had been pent up, dormant, a kind of growl. I looked back at CJ who was just getting on his board, watching my weird display. "Come on, bastard!" I said and he smiled and went hard to catch up with me.

Five

DAD AND I HADN'T BEEN TALKING MUCH, and he was still sleeping through most of his off time. I tried to remember the last time we'd had a proper conversation about anything and I couldn't remember one more recent than almost a year ago, before the shuttle explosion. The whole tone of the house was different now, and it occurred to me that Dad wasn't really talking to anyone. When he was home he was either sleeping or drinking Michelob (the only beer he ever drank) and brooding.

One Friday evening I came home from skating with CJ and he was asleep on the living room couch. I gestured to CJ to be quiet and we walked with our skateboards under arm to the kitchen where my mom was stirring a pot of something that smelled peppery. She looked up at us and smiled.

"What's up?" she said.

"Nothing. What's in the pot?"

She lifted out the wooden spoon and, with one hand held under it to catch the drippings she brought it over to my mouth and I sipped the broth.

"Needs salt."

"Like you'd know."

"It's really good, mom. Hey, can I stay at CJ's tonight?"

"That's fine. Your father's home tonight." She didn't like me to go to sleepovers if he was at the fire station.

I gave her a quick oafish hug and kissed her on the head.

"On your way out wake your father, please. It's going to take a couple times to get him up."

We went to my room first and I got a change of clothes, put it in a backpack, and walked out to the living room. My dad lay there on the couch on his back with one leg hiked up over the back of it, hands folded over his chest as if he'd fallen asleep while looking at a painting.

I touched his shoulder and whispered, "Dad…" His eyes opened a little and he grimaced. It looked like he saw me, but his eyes looked weird, very glazed. He unfolded his arms and swung a left hook at me. I moved back, just missed being caught on the chin by my father's massive fist.

"Dad!" I yelled, and he sat up and looked around, as if he'd just realized where he was. He stared at me, blinking.

"What happened?" he said.

"I just touched your shoulder and you swung at me."

"Yeah, well," he said. "Don't do that." He stood up and walked right by me and down the hall into his room.

I looked at CJ and he got in a boxer's pose and jabbed at me and then laughed. "That was messed up, man!"

***

When we got back to CJ's, the house was empty. We went to the kitchen, downed glasses of water, got snack cakes and went to his room. We sat around for a while, listening to music and talking about what we were going to do that night. We settled on skateboarding behind the Goodings grocery store where they had a ramped loading dock. After that, we'd play it by ear. Maybe we'd go back to his place and watch James Bond movies. Maybe we'd go skate somewhere else. We hoped something unplanned for would happen. We were game for whatever.

**

After skating around town until almost midnight, we ended up back at CJ's house. We raided the kitchen. We devoured anything that did not require more than a quick spin in the microwave; cookies, snack cakes and leftover pizza. After that we went into the living room and played *Ms. Pac-Man*. They had a full-size arcade version in their living room, and it was easy to find yourself in the middle of a marathon high-score war with whoever was around.

By one-thirty we were about to wrap things up when Natalie crept in through the front door. She held her index finger over her lips as she took big, quiet steps toward us.

"They asleep?" she whispered.

I nodded, and CJ pretended not to listen, and kept playing *Ms. Pac-man*.

Natalie grabbed the joystick and pulled down. CJ took a hand off and pushed his sister back. She lost her balance and fell into me and I reached up to steady her. My hand landed on her breast and I quickly let go. Consequently, she kept falling and I lost my balance and we collapsed on the floor. Natalie was on top of me. She got up onto her knees, sitting on top of me. She had a smirk on her face.

"See what happens when you let go?" she said.

She got up and walked over to her brother and made like she was going to punch him, and he flinched. She turned and walked away.

"Fucker!" he said. "I was about to break your high score."

She put her hand on the doorknob of her room door and looked directly at me. "I'm *so* sorry you didn't get to *score*." Then she disappeared into her room, but without closing the door.

"Dude," I whispered. "Was your sister flirting with me?"

"Probably. She flirts with everyone. She's a whore."

"Why does everyone think their sisters are whores?"

CJ didn't respond and walked into his room. I followed. We had to walk by Natalie's room to go to his. Her door was still open, and she was lying on her double bed, the lights off, watching TV, which cast a dim bluish light on everything. "Good night," she cooed, as we walked by.

Six

I T SEEMS MY SUCCESSFUL THIEVERY OF SAM'S dad's money had emboldened me because I started stealing money in earnest. If I saw an opportunity, I took it. If money was on the coffee table, I took it. If I went into my parents' room and saw a few bucks on a dresser, I took it. If I was at someone's house and they had been stupid enough to leave some cold cash in plain sight, I took it. I wasn't the slightest bit worried about getting caught, or of the repercussions of getting caught. It wasn't that I was brave or bold, I just didn't think about it. It wasn't at all like I was thinking, "Yeah, I might get caught, but who gives a shit." I just wasn't thinking at all. It went more like this: "There's money. Take it." Not the least bit consideration of repercussions. Not the first peripheral thought. Total inconsideration. Complete impetuous disregard. In retrospect, it seems borderline sociopathic. I was becoming a devious little shit. I thought of no one, really, but myself. I wanted. I wanted money. I wanted new stuff. I wanted to be able to go to the movies. I wanted girls to let me see their naked bodies. I wanted my parents to leave me alone. What I lacked in body hair I made up for in pure, unadulterated self-centeredness. There was one essential person in the world: me. If you could not do something for me, or push forward a desire of mine, you did not exist. There's nothing special about this—it's one of the commonest attitudes in the world—but that doesn't make it any less pathetic.

Anyway, I was becoming a junior league asshole. And it would turn out that I had perfect company. CJ, precocious as he was, had long ago become a solid second or third degree junior league asshole. I just had to follow my instincts and follow his example. He'd always been nice to me for some reason, and he'd usually give a person a chance, but if he decided he didn't like you, you were in for it.

I was finally starting to thin out a little, and had even grown an inch or two, so my ego fed off of those minor gains. Many victims lay in the swells and voids of my wake. James, my little brother, was one of the most significant. Just as my father was beginning to ignore both of us, I aggravated the situation, by following suit. I was a smaller, thinner, less hairy version of my dad. Dad ignored James and me, and I ignored everyone I couldn't use—and what's more useless than a little brother? James, consequently, had no one but my mom. And she had no one but him.

***

I saw a lot of CJ that school year and into the summer. It seems like all we did was skateboard all day, every day. But we did a lot of other things too. We went to the movies and went flying in CJ's dad's Cessna. We went rafting in the river. We shoplifted and went to the beach a few times. CJ and I were tight, and I thought often of Natalie. After that first night at CJ's, when she seemed to be flirting with me, I didn't see her again until the last week of the summer between seventh and eighth grades. She'd gone to visit some family in Virginia, a cousin and aunt, I believe. I anticipated her return, and annoyed the hell out of CJ about it. I felt like I actually had a chance with her. Not because she found me attractive or liked me, but because she was adventurous and flirtatious. She was what some might call a good sport. She was game for whatever. I stayed the night over CJ's on Natalie's first night back in town.

CJ's parents were gone most of the night, so it felt like a perfect set-up. We got to CJ's house at around eight that night, after skating all afternoon and evening, and did our usual thing—went straight to the kitchen. There was a pizza box sitting on the stove. "Yes!" said CJ, and he opened it, revealing four beautiful, glistening slices of pepperoni. "Two each," said CJ, and he grabbed the box and brought it into the living room where Natalie was sitting on the couch watching a movie. She wore cut-off jean shorts, a faded Van Halen 1984 shirt (the one with the cigarette-smoking angel with slicked back James Dean hair on the front of it) and her hair, almost buzz-cut short now, was her naural black color. She watched us sit down and begin eating the pizza, then she went back to watching.

"So," I said, "how was Virginia?"

"It was… Virginia." She was apathetically chewing some neon green Extra, reminding me of Hillary. I was a little beside myself. She put her finger to her lips and whispered, "Quiet…"

"I've never been to Virginia," I said, ignoring her command. "I've never been out of Florida, actually."

She smiled and whispered, "Aw, our little Florida Boy." A commercial came on and she got up and got her purse, which had been hanging on the back of a dining room chair. She sat back down and pulled a pack of Merit Ultra Lights out and lit one. I watched her the whole time. It occurred to me, at that moment, that the reason I felt like I had a chance with Nat was because she wasn't beautiful—unlike Hillary, who was uncommonly attractive. Nat was merely cute. She had big expressive brown eyes but her ears, which stood out on the side of her head, were probably a little too big and her butt was sort of flat and she had some acne. And she was very short. Probably only about five-feet tall. But, still, there was something about her. Something a little melancholy, but open, too. Something elfin. Despite her being older than me by two years, I felt like I had a chance with her. I felt like I was falling for her.

She threw the pack of cigarettes at me. It landed on my chest.

"Have one," she said.

I looked over at CJ. He shrugged and popped pizza crust in his mouth.

I picked up the pack and opened the hinged top and smelled inside. The smell reminded me of my dad—he smoked Winstons. I took one out and closed the box and put it on the coffee table. She threw me her Bic lighter and I lit the cigarette and puffed on it. I wasn't a complete novice. I'd done it before, at Sam's, and a couple times since, but it wasn't something I enjoyed.

"Take small drags," she said. "It's harsh at first."

I tried to do as she suggested. But I just didn't really like anything about it. It tasted lethal and the smoke hurt my throat. My Coke helped. I'd take a drag and then take a sip. Smoking was almost pleasant that way.

"So what are you hip dudes doing with the rest of your evening?" She stood up and walked over closer to us, sat on the coffee table. She was very close to me. She put her cigarette out and took mine out of my hand and started smoking it.

"I don't know," said CJ. "Watch some TV. Listen to music. What do you care?"

She put my cigarette out and then squeezed in between us on the couch. She put her hand on my leg. CJ sighed and got up.

"I'll be in my room, man," he said.

I didn't respond and Nat scooted over a little now that CJ was gone.

"He's my brother," she said, "but he's an asshole."

Her hand moved down some as she spoke.

"Yeah," I said, but that was all. I wasn't sure what to do or say. I didn't want to say or do anything, to be honest. I just wanted to sit there and be there with Nat. But that was all I could really envision—sitting there with her.

After a moment of awkward silence she picked the TV remote up, turned on the TV and flipped through the channels. She put MTV on. *The Cure* was on, *Fascination Street*. She sang along a little and then put her hand right between my legs without looking at me. I stopped breathing. I froze. She rubbed her hand around and then she turned and looked at me. I lifted a hand and put it on her breast. It was all I knew to do, my sad only move. She sighed a little. "Follow me," she said. She got up and turned and looked at me. "Come on." She waved a hand at me. I didn't want to get up for obvious reasons. She turned and started walking and disappeared into her room. I got up and followed behind her.

She turned a lamp on by her bed that had a blue lightbulb in it. She put a cassette tape in her stereo, *The Smiths*, and then she lay down on her bed and patted at a spot in front of her. "Close the door first," she said. "And lock it."

"What about CJ?" I said.

"He'll be fine," she said.

I heard music coming from his room. *Danzig,* "She Rides".

I got in bed with her, on top of the covers. Her room smelled good. She smelled good. She had a clean, floral smell about her and I wanted to lick it off of her, but I was also too scared to do anything. She seemed so sophisticated. She turned over so that she was facing the wall. "Spoon me," she said.

"What?"

"Scoot over and lay next to me, as close as you can get. Put your body against mine."

I did as she asked.

"Put your arm around me."

I did, again, as she asked, and she took my hand and pulled it down to her side; my forearm was just under her breasts. She had taken her bra off, without my realizing it, and her breasts, through her shirt material, touched my arm, if a touch could be a whisper.

"Move in closer," she said.

I did.

"That's it," she said and she pushed her ass into me and moved it back and forth.

"Don't worry," she said. "We won't do anything more than this. I know you're nervous."

"Okay," I said. It was wonderful, just lying there like that. Feeling each other's bodies and saying nothing and listening to the music.

"Can I tell you something?" she said once a song finished.

I told her sure, moved my hand to her side, to her hip and thigh, and began caressing her. It felt like a familiarity I'd won.

"My mother and my brother hate me. My dad is the

only one in this house who loves me."

I hadn't expected that kind of frankness from her, especially about something so seemingly out-of-the-way of this moment. But maybe it wasn't. Maybe our intimacy brought it on.

"My dad almost punched me the other day." I hadn't thought about saying it, and perhaps it was somewhat dishonest to say it the way I'd said it, but I felt like commiserating with her. I felt like adding to the intimacy an immediacy of the moment.

She turned her head back, just a bit, to try to see my face, and then she laid her head back into her pillow. We were quiet for a while, listening to Morrissey sing about how ridiculous and sad life could be. The tape stopped and I listened to our breathing, our rhythmic breathing, and the faint sound of the music coming from CJ's room. I felt like I was betraying him somewhat. As good as this was, I knew I needed to get back to him. I started thinking of ways to make an exit, excuses. Before I could come up with something, she turned her body around and she was lying on her back now, my arm around her at the waist. She looked up at me and put her hand on my head and moved some hair around. "I'll have sex with you, white boy," she said. "Not tonight, but some other time. If you decide you want to, I'll do it."

"Have you had sex before?" I said.

She smiled and kept moving my hair around, like she was putting it in some kind of order. "Yes."

"With who?" I moved her shirt up so that I could see her belly. Her bellybutton was very cute to me, an innie. Her stomach was perfectly pudgy.

"A few different guys."

"Anyone I know?"

"God, no!" she said. "Older guys. You wouldn't

know any of them. One was in Virginia, anyway." She pulled her shirt down and I put my hand on her hip again.

"Do you think I'm fat?"

"No! I hope you don't think you are. That's ridiculous if you do."

"Give me a kiss," she said.

I leaned in and touched my lips to hers and she grabbed the back of my head and she stuck her tongue in my mouth and we kissed like that for a long time, with tongues and all. It was my first time, and it was like I was in some kind of perfect place. After a while she pushed me slightly away and said, let's go back to spooning, and we did, and we fell asleep that way.

When I woke up the next morning she was gone.

***

A few weeks later, just into the new school year, Natalie got shipped back up to Virginia for good. She'd been caught having sex with one of her dad's employees, a tiler named Roger, a surfer-dude in his late twenties. I'd met him a few times, and that somewhat made it more real for me. He was a stoner, beach bum guy, with long sun-bleached hair and a tribal tattoo on his shoulder. She had been my sure thing, and now she was gone. And it was all his fault.

"I wish I could go back to Virginia too," said CJ, after he told me about it all. He was putting new Independent trucks on a brand new Vallely skateboard.

"I don't," I said. "That would suck for me."

"Man, Natalie is such a slut. She would still be here right now if she could keep her legs together." He seemed sad she was gone.

"She told me your dad was the only one who cared about her, and that you and your mom hated her."

"That's bullshit. She's always saying shit like that." He smirked. "Did you do it with her? That night when you stayed over?"

"Nah. We did stuff, but we didn't do it."

CJ finished tightening all the bolts on his skateboard and trucks, then flipped it over and stood on it. Shifted back and forth.

"Let's go up to Goodings and skate the loading dock."

***

Things were getting weirder at home. My dad was rarely there now and when he wasn't asleep he seemed very distracted. Mom walked around the house like a cat, nervous and cautious, like something was going to jump out at her. James seemed fine—the same annoying little shit as always. I didn't give any of this much thought, being a self-centered bastard, but there was a strange mood in the house.

Being an eighth grader now instead of a newbie seventh grader had its perks. I was picked on less. I'd gotten a little taller over summer break and had lost some of the baby fat I'd apparently had. A new kid, from Valdosta, Georgia, named Sean Helm, was in my homeroom. He was pretty cool, had a southern accent and a beat up Jeff Grosso he rode to school and stuck in his locker. Most of us did that—kept our boards in our lockers. Sean and CJ (a seventh grader now) and I became tight. We all lived on the same side of town and we'd skate to school together. School was pretty good, too—so good, in fact, that there just isn't much to report. I was left alone, had no bully, and made acceptable grades—C's and B's. The year progressed without incident until the last three months.

***

Philip Normandy was small, probably five-two when he first woke up in the morning. At lunch one day in mid-April I told him about this trick Sean Helm had brought down with him from Valdosta. You'd bend over with your hands on your knees, take twenty-four breaths (to this day I have no idea why it had to be twenty-four) and then stood up straight with your arms crossed over your chest and held your breath. Someone was supposed to come up from behind you and pick you up and count to three and put you back down, gently, and nine out of ten times you'd be passed out unconscious by the time they put you down. Sean did it to me and it had worked and I woke up on the gym floor with a pounding headache and a ring of seventh and eighth graders around me with big grins on their faces.

"It's so crazy, man! You have to try it."

"Is it safe?" said Phil, which should have been a red flag. Phil didn't have the spirit for this kind of thing, but I was too pumped to try it on someone and Phil was kind of a pushover, and he was in my Art II class, which was right after lunch, so I pressed on.

We had ten minutes between lunch ending and art class beginning, so we went straight to art classroom because we knew no one, not even Mrs. Freud, would be in there. She was a heavy smoker and used every chance she got to go grab a smoke.

"All right," I said, "lean over and take twenty-four breaths, like I told you before."

By about breath twenty Bruce Lamont had walked up. He stood next to me.

"I know what you're doing."

I told him to shut up and made sure Phil stood up straight with his arms crossed and his breath held, and I got up behind him and picked him up and held him tight for about three seconds and then gently put him down. But his legs did not give. I let go of him and walked around and looked at his face. His eyes were open, but he had a stunned look on his face, like he'd just shit himself. While Bruce and I stood there staring at him his body folded at the waist and he hit the ground head first and started convulsing.

"Oh shit!" I said and bent down and touched Phil on the arm. "Phil! Phil!" I shook him gently and he came to. He looked around the room and then he squealed a little and held his head. Saliva came pouring, like blood, out of his mouth. "Phil," I said, "Can you get up."

"What happened?" He was sitting now. Kids started to show up for class, but still no Mrs. Freud.

"We tried to do the pass-out thing and I thought it didn't work on you, but it did, and I didn't catch you. I'm sorry, man. You really looked wide awake."

"My head is killing me."

"You got a shiner from where you hit the ground. Plus you have a bad headache when you wake up. That's normal."

A cute but obnoxiously perfect girl named Erica Horne walked up.

"What's going on here?"

"Go away, Erica," I said.

Phil said, "Hi, Erica," in a really weird, dreamy tone.

"Something's wrong with Phil," she said. "You should go see Dean Guthrie."

"We are," I said. "Will you tell Mrs. Freud when she gets here?"

***

Mr. Guthrie did not fuck around. He was a Vietnam veteran

who smoked cigars and doled out some pretty twisted punishments. He once made Chris Garrity lick his own spit off a wall. He made me and Andre Fortney run until one of us 'couldn't run anymore', which ended up meaning once Andre started sobbing uncontrollably. I knew I was in some seriously deep shit. I'd already been to his office so many times this year (for ignorant shit, like farting loudly in class and shooting spitballs at the chalkboard) that he'd told me if I came again I would get three-days suspension. I walked, holding onto Phil, and thinking about how pissed my parents were going to be if I got suspended. Plus Phil still didn't quite seem right. It seemed like a part of him was still unconscious.

Guthrie's door was propped open, as it usually was. He was seated at his desk.

"What do we have here?" he said. He let us linger in the limbo of his office's threshold for a moment, as if he enjoyed the look of us standing there. Finally, he said, "Have a seat, gentleman," leaned back in his chair, which issued a strained squeak, and put his arms up behind his head. "This oughta be good." The dean and I were familiar, so he pointed at me. "Let's start with you, Wingnut." I told him what had happened. I was very detailed. I didn't lie. I started with Sean (without naming him) and ended with us walking to the dean's office. The dean could sense, I believe, that we were both extremely rattled by the whole business. The dean pointed at Phil. "Has jughead here told the whole truth and nothing but the truth?" Phil nodded. "That's what happened," he added. "I mean, I think. I don't know what happened during the time I was unconscious."

The dean looked down, like he was looking at a wounded animal nestled in his lap, and then looked up at us. "It takes two to tango," he said. He wrote us tardy slips and told us to go to class.

"That's it, sir?" I said.

He sighed. "That's it. But, I swear to god—if I see your stupid face one more time I'm calling your parents and giving you three days. You hear me?"

"Loud and clear, sir."

Phil and I quietly walked back to class. I was both relieved and disappointed. I guess I felt like I should have got some kind of punishment—something. Nothing seemed wrong. "It takes two to tango," seemed like a cop out, a load of crap, like he was being lazy and didn't feel like trying to come up with a punishment to fit the crime, like he wasn't up for calling our parents. Before opening the door to class, I turned to Phil, my hand on the doorknob. "Hey, I'm real sorry, man. That went all wrong."

"It's okay," said Phil. "It's like the dean said. Took both of us. I'm to blame too." We both smiled a little and I slapped Phil on the shoulder, but none of it felt right.

Seven

THE SCHOOL YEAR ALMOST OVER NOW, I found myself near the threshold of another big transition. Next year, ninth grade, and kings of the campus again. Sean Helm and I would be fucking tops, and CJ would be in the eighth grade. We were moving our way up the social ladder. We weren't top tier, but we were close. Sean and CJ were both really good at skating, and I was coming along. Girls were taking notice. I saw nothing but smooth sailing ahead. I was wrong—which is usually the case in these smooth-sailing type situations.

The Nooch came back, and they'd put him in the seventh grade. They were going to try catching him up so that he could transition to ninth grade next year. But this whole situation clearly pissed him off. He was different now, angrier and desperate. I hadn't seen him in a while, and he'd grown taller, but he was skinnier now. The accident and his recovery had clearly been a physical and emotional strain on him, and it looked like it still strained him. Something, it seemed, had been sucked out of him. His eyes had a crazy glint. His first day back he came up to me at my locker.

"Don't think I forgot about you, asshole," he whispered. He stood behind me. I turned around. All I could think to say was, how you doing?

"Better than you," he said, which was kind of pathetic. Clearly, I was doing better than he was. It was posturing, an attempt to regain what he once had. I realized I wasn't scared of him anymore. He was different now, sure, but so was I. I was older, taller, and I had some good friends now. People noticed me.

"Things have changed around here while you were convalescing, Georgie Boy. You're trying to do something that ain't happening anymore." I shouldered him away from me so that I could move out into the hall and walk to class. He started laughing—he laughed like he'd heard the funniest joke ever. I kept walking. The laughing stopped and the hallway went eerily quiet. Suddenly I was yanked back and down to the ground, and in an instant he was standing over me, straddling me. He bent over and put his finger in my face. He was smiling and his eyes were huge.

"Nothing's changed, man. Everything is exactly the same, and you're the same little pussy you've always been. You understand?"

Holy shit! He was right. Suddenly I was petrified. It was just like before. Nothing had changed. I did not respond, and thankfully I heard a voice, a teacher's voice.

"Nucci!"

He took off running. I slowly got up. The Dean was standing next to me.

"You and Nucci—still at it…"

"He started it, Dean. I was minding my own business—I swear." The back of my head hurt where he'd grabbed my hair to yank me down.

The Dean told me to come with him.

"Don't worry, I'm just gonna write you a tardy pass."

He knew that George and I had had a bully-victim relationship, so he went easy on me. "Understand," he said, "there ain't a whole lot I can do to him right now—in terms of punishment. You know what happened to him, right? The car accident?"

I told him that I did.

"Little jerk almost died. We'll get him. But we'll have to wait, maybe till next year. In the meantime, try to avoid him."

Avoiding George wouldn't be too hard. He was still a seventh grader, so our classes were in different parts of the school. I just had to keep an eye out at lunch and gym.

***

I got home from school that day, the day George returned to school, and I could tell immediately that something was going on. Music was playing on the living room stereo and the house was very tidy looking. "Mom!" I said and she responded that she was in the bedroom. Her voice sounded light and cheerful. I walked down the hall and as I got closer I could hear her talking to someone, but I couldn't make out what they were saying. It was a man's voice, and it sounded familiar, but I could not place it. The bedroom door was open. I slowly walked up and peeked around the corner. I was startled to find my dad sitting on their bed, talking with her—and then the fact that I was startled to find my dad right where he belonged freaked me out. I realized it had been quite some time since I'd heard him talking like this with someone, like a normal person.

"Hey!" they said in unison.

I took my backpack off and leaned on the doorframe.

"How was school, bud?" My dad had a weird, but not unpleasant, glow about him. It was nice to have him talking to me.

"Fine," I lied.

"Have a seat," he said, pointing to the small chair next to the door. "We have something to tell you."

I had a tendency to clam up in situations like these, so that's what I did. I just sat there waiting for whatever he was going to say. I didn't know what to expect.

"We have decided," he started slowly, glancing over at my mom, "that we're going to make a change." He smiled. He seemed proud of himself to have made it that far.

I did not respond. I waited for the rest.

"A move, to be exact," mom chimed in.

"We're moving?" I said.

"Yes. We're moving to Summerdale." They both paused, waited for me to respond, with huge smiles on their faces, as if Summerdale was the best place ever. To be honest, I had mixed emotions about Summerdale. Summerdale was in central Florida, almost exactly central. Right in the middle. It's where my dad had grown up. Almost all of my relatives on my dad's side lived there, generations of them, and they almost all worked in some facet of the citrus industry—fruit pickers, fruit haulers, packinghouse workers, grove owners, juice plant employees. Working class, rural people these. Summerdale was largely a poor area. It was completely different from where we lived now—coastal and suburban and middle class. To be honest, I was more confused than anything else. I loved going to Summerdale when we went there to visit. I loved how different it was— like visiting a different country almost, but I couldn't imagine why we'd move there. In a way it seemed like a step down.

All I could think to say was, "Really?"

They looked at each other and laughed nervously, as if they understood my bewilderment, but didn't want to admit it.

"Yes," my mom said, "*Really.*"

My dad just kept smiling, and he nodded along to what my mom said. He seemed speechless himself.

"We just think," she went on, putting a hand on my dad's leg, "that it's time for a change. Something new."

"Summerdale is nothing *new*," I said.

"But we've never lived there," she said.

"Think of it as an experiment," said dad. "If it doesn't work out, we come back."

Could it be that simple? I wondered. I thought about what Nooch had said, in the hallway—nothing's changed. Things change but they don't change. Maybe we'll be in a different location, but we'll still be the same people.

"When?" I said. "When do we start packing?"

"Now, I guess." My mom looked over at my dad.

"Yes," he said. "We will move some time during the first few weeks of summer vacation. After school's over. I have a house lined up for us. It's vacant and we can get there whenever we get there."

"Does James know yet?"

"Yes," said mom. "He said that he can't wait to pick fruit with uncle Corley. Isn't that hysterical!" She laughed a little too much and dad got up, so I stood up too. He walked over to me and messed my hair and patted me on the shoulder. "Think of it as an adventure," he said. His voice almost seemed to be pleading with me and his eyes now looked a little sad. I smiled and nodded. "Okay," I said. "It will be an adventure."

Mom cheered, "Yay!" and I picked up my backpack and went into my room and lay on my bed thinking about this really huge development that my parents seemed to be treating like it was no big deal.

**

This whole moving thing seemed like a waste to me. I'd come a long way, socially. I wasn't a little grommet anymore. I was on my way to a certain degree of popularity. But moving would change all of that, wouldn't it? I'd have to start all over again. There'd be no Nooch, though. That was a plus. But who's to say that there won't be another Nooch—maybe even someone worse.

On Monday, during first period, I sat and weighed things out, the pros and cons of moving, while Mr. Cahill talked away about something math-related. It was the final week of school. All of my classes had gotten a little smaller. Grades were in already and everyone knew that the last week of school was bullshit. Lots of families had already begun their summer trips. My summer trip would last forever. I wouldn't be coming back. For the first time I felt sad. The classroom door opened and Phil Normandy slowly peeked his head in and Cahill waved at him and pointed to his vacant seat. Phil slinked in, almost on tiptoes, and sat down. He got up and walked a slip of paper, probably a tardy slip, to Cahill. Cahill glanced at it, smiled at Phil, and put the slip in his pocket.

When Phil sat down, I looked at him till he looked my way. I made a face—stuck my tongue out and put my hands around my neck, like I was being choked. He cracked a one-sided smile, and then looked away.

I sat with Sean and CJ at lunch, but I kept looking for Phil. He had the same lunch and would sometimes sit with us. I never saw him. We all made plans to meet up at CJ's after school, and then go to The Church to skate a new funbox somebody had brought up there.

**

My last class was nowhere near my locker, so after the last bell rang, I walked all the way to the other side of school to get my board. It's funny how quickly school clears out I thought as I got to my locker. I dialled in the lock number and opened it. Nothing was in my locker now but my board—no books, no supplies—nothing. I reached in to pull my board out and I got an eerie feeling. I turned around and Phil Normandy stood there with a vacant expression.

"Dude! You scared the shit out of me!" I looked around. It was quite. No one seemed to be around but me and Phil. I shut my locker and started walking. Phil walked with me.

"What's up, man?" I said.

"I'm not doing so well." He scratched his head. He walked in a somewhat stooped, forward-leaning posture. It seemed like a new thing to me, like a new style. His eyes were glassy. He's been crying, I thought.

"What do you mean?"

"Somebody told me something—the day we did the pass-out thing, you know."

"Oh, no. What?"

"It causes a bubble in your brain." He touched his head and looked at me with his glassy eyes. "Did you know that?"

"What?"

"Yeah. And the bubble just sort of floats around in there until it eventually pops, which could be in a few days or a few years. But when it does—when it pops—you die. Did you know this? I didn't know this?"

"Phil, that's total bullshit. We've all done it and none

of us have died. That's the biggest load of crap. If that was true it would be on the news and everyone would know about it and your parents would constantly be talking about it. Someone's just trying to scare you. Who told you that, anyway?"

He didn't answer. By now we'd reached the sidewalk and we kept walking together. I knew where he lived. His house was on the way to where I was going, to The Church.

"Are you saying I'm stupid or something?" He looked like he was about to cry.

"No, Phil. You're one of the smartest people I know. You're in all advanced classes. I just think—I don't know. I wish none of this had happened. I'm sorry it happened."

"I know you are. I know you didn't mean to hurt me." He looked down and kept walking in this new slumped over way, like his heart wasn't in it.

"Phil," I said. "You're gonna be okay. Don't listen to—whoever told you that."

"It doesn't matter. It's probably not true. But, anyway, I feel different now."

I walked the whole way to Phil's house with him. We didn't say another word to each other until we reached his house and I said bye and he said, see you later, with a pathetic little wave of his hand, then I got on my board and skated fast the rest of the way to The Church.

***

Over the years The Church's parking lot had become a real destination, and had accrued lots of ramps and boardslides and boxes and kids would come from all over the county to skate there. Even a few sponsored guys frequented the place. It was the closest thing we had to a skate park.

By the time I arrived Sean and CJ were already there.

A couple of other guys, high schoolers, were there too. One was this guy named Derek who was really, really good and we ended up sitting on a parking block watching him skate until he and his buddy left. We piddled around, did what we could do, which didn't seem like much after watching Derek. CJ was the best of the three of us, then Sean. Sean wasn't much better than me, but he looked better doing what he could do. I still had a somewhat awkward way about me. Sean and CJ looked fluid and comfortable on their boards. How you look doing something matters almost as much as being able to do it at all. Plus CJ always had a new board. He'd buy a board, skate it for no more than six months, then buy a new one. Sean and I weren't so lucky. Our parents weren't as well off as CJ's and we were all still too young to get a job of any kind, other than mowing lawns, which none of us wanted to do. We weren't industrious enough for that. We just wanted to skateboard and listen to music and be jackasses. Anyway, Sean and I had old, falling apart trucks, boards with chipped tales, and badly coned tires, while CJ had all this nice stuff.

But the board I had now was the best one I'd had for a while. It was a Ray Barbee. It had a nice shape and I was doing my best skating ever on it. I'd gotten it as a hand-me-down from CJ. He'd gotten it and only rode it for about two weeks because he just couldn't get used to it. He gave it to me. I ended up loving it. It was still in good shape and had lots of tail left—no chips. I had pretty new wheels now too. I had traded my comic book collection to Geoff for an almost brand new set of Vision Blurs. He'd gotten into skating briefly and then gone back to his nerdy, indoor ways. I had moved out of that clique and didn't plan on returning, so it had been a fair swap.

It was starting to get dark out, about seven-thirty. I had to be home by eight-thirty. We saw someone skating up the road, headed toward The Church, but couldn't make out who it was until he got to the far side of the parking lot. It was George.

He stopped and looked at all three of us. Sean and CJ knew who he was, but George didn't really know them. But he could see that they were with me.

"What's up, dudes?" he said in a not too friendly way. He was wearing surfing baggies and slip-on Vans, but wasn't wearing a shirt.

"Never knew you skated," I said.

"I guess I'm giving it a try," he said. "I'm not allowed to start surfing again yet. I guess this," he gave the board a push with his foot, "is the next best thing."

"Dude," said CJ, "that board is ancient." It was an old Vision Gator—super flat and thick, looked like it weighed ten pounds.

George looked down at it and then looked at CJ, who was smiling and holding his board under his arm. George shrugged off the comment and gave the board a push and started carving around the lot. He rode the thing like it was a surfboard, in a very old-school style. Sean pushed over to the boardslide and started skating it. I just stood there, watching George. CJ started mocking George, carving big loops in the lot and bending his body into the turns and saying, "Dude! Bro! Shaka Bra!" as he went along. "Totally gnarly! Totally tubular! Whoa! Cowabunga bro!"

George stopped and watched CJ. CJ pushed over to where I was standing and stopped, stood next to me. He nudged me with his elbow and winked at me.

"What the fuck are you doing?" I whispered. "You trying to get my ass kicked?"

"He's not gonna do nothing," said CJ. "Three against one, dude."

George pushed over to where we were standing and

stopped.

I remembered Phil. "Hey, man. Did you tell Phil he has a bubble in his brain and if it pops he'll die?"

He didn't answer.

"If you did, that was a dick move. He believed you. He's all fucked up now."

"I didn't say shit. He's a pathetic dork."

"Dude, put on a fucking shirt," said CJ. By now Sean was standing in the circle with the rest of us and he busted out laughing. "Totally, Shaka-Bra!" He laughed some more.

George smiled and rubbed his chest. "You're just jealous," he said. Even though he'd gotten thin from the accident he did still have a surfer's chiseled physique.

CJ, unexpectedly, whipped his shirt off, tucked it into the waistline of his shorts, and started carving around the parking lot again, yelling Cowabunga and shit. We all laughed, even George. CJ came back and stopped in front of George and pounded his chest and let out a kind of Tarzan cry. We all laughed again. George just stood there smiling. I was loving it, seeing him on the other end of things, being bullied and made fun of. Things have changed after all, I thought. George wasn't going to be able to treat me the same as before.

He picked up his old, beat up skateboard, held it up. "You know, this thing is a piece of shit, you're right. It was my brother's, back when he used to skate. It's old school. You guys have nice, new boards. I've never even skated on one of these new school boards, with noses and all of that. Looks pretty bad ass." He pointed at mine. "Can I try yours out?"

I couldn't think of any reason not to let him. I pushed the board over to him and he jumped on it and carved around. "Nice!" he said. "I may have to get one of these." He rolled back to where we were standing and stopped. He pushed my board back and forth with his foot. He got back on it and pushed around. He got maybe twenty yards away and positioned the board right in front of him. He looked at me and smiled, then he jumped up and landed both feet squarely in the middle of my skateboard, snapping it in half, the grip tape the only thing holding the two halves together.

"Nothing's changed, pussy!" He picked up my skateboard and ripped it in half and threw the halves either side of him.

"Dude," said Sean. "that's fucked up."

I walked up to him and stood in front of him. "What the fuck is wrong with you, man? Why are you always doing shit like this?"

He put his finger on my chest. "You're what's wrong with me. I fucking hate you. You're such a piece of shit. Your existence makes me angry."

Before I could even think about it, I'd punched him in the stomach, as hard as I could. Then I hit him with a few more. I stepped back, expecting retaliation, but when I looked up, George had a big smile on his face. He laughed. "What was that?" He laughed some more. "So pathetic." He turned around, found his skateboard, and rode off.

"What an asshole," said Sean.

"Let me know when you want me to kick his ass," said CJ. "I'd love to do it."

"I don't need anyone to kick his ass. I could do it myself."

"Whatever you say," said CJ. "Looks like you need a new board."

"I fucking loved that board, man. God! I hate him."

CJ told me he was pretty sure he had a deck lying around somewhere that I could have. I knew he did. He always had a few decks stashed under his bed. I left CJ and

Sean at The Church and walked home with my broken board. I was so pissed and depressed that the idea of moving away was okay with me. I could use a change of scenery—a place where there was no George Nucci.

***

Nothing special happened—no big last hurrah. We loaded up the car, got in and drove away. I never even had a chance to say any proper goodbyes to anyone. James and I sat in the backseat of the Jeep Cherokee and looked out our separate windows. We watched the everyday world drift by and give way to something else. We'd been on these roads before, we'd gone this way before, but never like this, never this aware of what went by outside the window. For all we knew we were never coming back. This could be our last look at things. The cab of the car was quiet. No one spoke until we were on the highway, U.S. 192, well on our way, and far from the town. We all had mixed feelings about leaving and well into the vast mix of palmetto marsh and cattle ranches that stretched from extreme west Brevard County, through Osceola and into Lawrence County, where the scenery changed to cow pastures and citrus groves.

"Great song," said Dad. He reached for the volume nob and turned it up. Whenever we travelled we always listened to this 'Oldie Goldie' station that played music from the fifties, sixties and early seventies. It was the *Doors*, now, Jim Morrison singing 'Keep your eyes on the road and your hands upon the wheel.' My dad looked at me through the rear-view mirror and smiled.

"What do you think? A sign? A sign from Mr. Mojo Risin. We're on the right path." He tapped the wheel with the fat of his palm. His driving seemed to sync up with the throb of the songs rhythm. My mom shook her head and looked back at us, smiled and bit her bottom lip. James and I looked at each other and smiled too. We all sang the end together:

Let it roll, baby, roll!
Let it roll, baby, roll!
Let it roll, baby, roll!
Let it roll, all night long!

***

I felt better after that—we all did, I think. Whatever else, we were together and doing our own thing, as Dad would so often say. "Just do your own thing." It was a refrain of our childhood. What should I do, Dad? "Whatever you want. Do your own thing. Don't worry about anyone else." It sounded like something you couldn't argue with. It was an espousal of a certain very American way of living. Keep moving forward— 'roll, baby, roll' —and don't worry too much about anything or anyone, because it will all work out in the end—or it won't, but it doesn't ultimately matter all that much. Like all very simple things, it was alluring, and a little too easy—too easy because it ignored so much. But it was the closest thing he had to a philosophy. Anyway, that summer, we were 'doing our own thing' and there was no arguing that. And in that moment, singing ourselves down the highway, through swampland and cow pastures, it almost felt right. During the first year away from the only place I'd ever called home, whenever I thought too hard about all we'd left behind, whenever I felt some emotions creeping in, I would shrug it off. I'd think of us in the car together, singing our anthem, 'Let it roll, baby, roll' and barrelling towards our new lives, and I'd feel a little better.

{Part Two}

One

I STOOD IN THE COW PASTURE AND LOOKED UP AT the thing, sputtering and whining, as it slowly drifted across the sky. It coughed loudly and dropped a little, then regained its composure and picked back up again. A fine mist sprayed out the back of it.

"Dad, is that what I think it is?"

He pulled back the bolt of the .22 longshot. The shell flipped out, he inserted a new bullet, and looked up. "Cropduster."

"That's what I thought. I think this is the first time I've ever seen one in real life."

He handed me the rifle. "Except that one is seeding, not dusting. Can you see the bottle?"

The bottle was about fifty yards away, at the edge of the woods that were at the back of my uncle's pasture. "Seeding? You mean like dropping seeds down from a plane instead of planting them in the ground?

"Something like that. Shoot it."

I aimed, and pulled the trigger. The top of the bottle fell into the bottom of it.

"You blew the center clean out of it. Good job."

I looked back up at the sky and saw the plane circling back from a distance. It was good to be spending time with my dad.

***

He had a place lined up for us, but, as it turned out, it wouldn't be ready for another week. We stayed with my aunt and uncle: Corley and Twyla. I loved them. I'd always loved them. Twyla was kind and reserved and made the best biscuits and gravy I'd ever had. She was a redhead, with very light skin, and exactly five feet tall. Corley looked more like me and dad, dark brown hair —almost black—and skin that tanned easily. He was pretty short too, probably only about five-seven. He could be mean as hell, classic country orneryness, and he'd gladly whip your ass (all my aunts and uncles were implicitly allowed to whip each others' children) if he caught you doing something he thought was 'ignorant,' like something dangerous or destructive, but he was fun to be around. He liked to wrestle and goof around and he knew how to do so many things, and he didn't mind letting you tag along. They lived on a small farm, and he'd invite me along if he was going to do something he thought I might find interesting. "Boy," he'd say. "I'm gonna go shoot this hog over yonder. You coming?" Hell yes, I was coming! He was thoughtful, in this way. Coming from such a different place, being on that farm was always strange and wonderful for me, and he understood that. He could see the wonder just streaming out of me like sunrays. Their son, Willard, who was a year and a half older than I was, was fun too. He'd let me be his partner in crime. I guess this rubbed off on me a little, because I even started letting James hang out with us. I knew Will didn't care—he wasn't that type of guy. He didn't care how old a person was. Growing up in the country, on a farm, he didn't have a lot of ground rules. And company was company.

We'd put all our furniture and stuff in a storage unit and only brought our clothes to Corley and Twyla's. They had an extra room in their doublewide for our parents and James and I stayed with Will. As soon as we got all out stuff packed in, James and I took off with Will.

"Hold up," said Corley. "Where y'all headed to?"

"We're just going outside to mess around," said Will. He had a profound respect for his dad, and was careful what he said around him, even if he didn't always do what he was told. Consequently, he'd learned to make all explanations of his comings and goings as vague as possible, unless his father pressed him for details. It was a pretty sophisticated strategy for a boy of his age.

"Look here." He made eye contact with both of us. "Keep away from those goddamn chickens. I don't even want to see you chasing them." He eyed all three of us. James and I nodded.

"Yes sir," said Will.

Corley quickly grabbed me and put me in a headlock and started grinding his knuckles into my head.

He giggled, let go, and slapped me in the head. Will stood there smiling. "Git the hell outta here!"

We took off and out the door, and went straight to a small lean-to and walked inside of it. Will walked to the corner where something was covered up with a burlap sack. He glanced back and whipped it off. "This," he said, "is my secret weapon."

"Nice! Let's take it out in the woods and set up a

target."

Will looked at me like I'd asked him to eat a dog turd, then he looked over at James who stood and stared in awe at the thing.

"Do you know what this is?" He caressed the stock.

"A pellet rifle."

"No hell it ain't. It's the goddamn Chickenator."

"Dude, your dad said to leave the chickens alone." I said in a whisper.

"Dude," Will mocked, "he's not gonna find out. Check this out." He directed me to the corner of the lean-to nearest a wide-open area. Sun beamed through an oval-shaped hole in the joint. You could fit the rifle barrel into it and still see out of it. Sure as shit, some chickens were out there milling around.

"You really hate chickens, don't you?"

"Naw, it's just fun to shoot at 'em."

"I've never shot anything before," said James.

Chickens have got to be some of the dumbest creatures alive. We'd pop one, and it would squawk, but it would hardly move. It would stay right there in the general area. We shot the same one several times without it doing much more than taking a few quick steps in one direction, then the other. I started to feel bad for the damn things. It got boring real quick.

"Will," I said, "let's find something else to do. This ain't really worth a possible ass-whupping from your dad, is it?"

He put the rifle down and sighed. "I can't wait for Junior to get back home."

"Who's Junior?"

"Lives next door." Next door meant the ten-acre plot that was next to theirs. They had cattle—not just chickens and a couple pigs and filthy dogs—and Junior was reputed to do some pretty spectacular things with the cattle—weird, circus-freak stuff. "He'll be back in a few weeks. Went to visit some family or something for the summer."

"Well, I wished you had someplace to skateboard."

Will's eyes lit up. "We do."

"You don't have a skateboard."

"Hell, yes, I do!"

James kicked the dirt. "I'm going inside and watch TV." He hated skateboarding. "Let me know," he said, as he walked off, "if you start shooting at chickens again."

We hustled over to a small shed behind their trailer and Will opened it up. He dug through piles and stacks of shit for about ten minutes until he said, "Hold up. Here it is," and pulled out from the back a K-Mart special. It had Bubbalicious pink wheels and the deck was florescent green. The grip tape was peeling around the edges and for graphics it had this stupid Court Jester face on it. It was a total hunk of shit, but I didn't say so. I knew he didn't know what to do with it anyway.

"Cool," I said. "Let me go grab my board."

We walked down a dirt road, passed Junior's property, and down further passed a plot of land that had nothing on it. We passed a broken-down school bus with streaks of black mold and green scum all over it. The bus had makeshift curtains in its windows.

"Dude, what the hell?"

"That's the Baggetts' place."

"They live in a bus?"

"Yeah." Will didn't seem to think that was strange. "They're a bunch of assholes. They're gone this time of year."

"I guess living in a bus would turn you into an asshole." In what would be the front yard of the bus stood rows of plants I took to be a garden.

"Naw, it ain't just that. The kids get beat on and the folks is drunk all the time."

"Where are they? Seems deserted now."

"They'll be back in a few weeks. They're migrants. They're up in Michigan or somewheres now. Picking apples, I think. They'll be back soon for citrus harvest. Consider yourself lucky that you'll probably be gone when they get back. They's three boys and a girl, and every one of them is mean as hell."

Man, I thought. This is a whole different world than the one I was used to living in, at the beach. Migrant workers and people living in a bus. My dad had told me stories of stuff like this, from his childhood, but I'd never really experienced it for myself until now. I'd for sure entered a new story. But I didn't feel part of it. I was an outsider looking in on all of it. I wasn't like Will. This shit was weird to me. It wasn't commonplace. Just seeing the plot of land with the bus on it filled me with a shaky urgent buzz. I felt like telling everyone I knew. I thought of CJ and Sean, and Sam, even. They wouldn't have believed this. Thinking about my old friends got me down. I wondered what they were doing.

Eventually we were standing in front of a slab of concrete about forty feet square.

"Here it is," said Will.

"Here what is?"

"A place where we can do some skateboarding."

I looked around. We were at the end of a dirt road. Clearly there had been something here once, maybe a convenience store or something, but now there was only this slab. For as far as the eye could see there was nothing but dirt and trees. The highway was about a quarter mile away, you could hear a truck swoosh by every so often, and that was asphalt, and I was sure I could skate up the highway to something better than this—a strip mall or bank, perhaps—but I didn't know how far. For now, this slab was it.

"It ain't much, is it?" I hopped on my board and pushed, and in a second I was on the other side of the slab. I thought again of CJ and Sean and felt a mix of sadness, jealousy and anger.

"Naw, it ain't. This ain't really skateboarding country." Will seemed a little embarrassed or disappointed.

"It'll have to do for now," I said. "You know how to Ollie?"

"What?"

I told him to put down his hunk of shit generic skateboard and come get on mine. And I taught him how to Ollie. No shit. In about one hour he got it. It had taken me a year to learn how to Ollie and here Will got the hang of it in under sixty minutes. He was a natural. It pissed me off. He was like a goddamn idiot savant of skateboarding and chicken harassment. Little fucker.

***

After three days of shooting chickens, and skateboarding on that little slab, I'd had about enough. Withdrawals had set in. I needed a different kind of wide openness. All this goddamn nature and rusticity had worn thin. I needed concrete and asphalt. So I took off down the highway, Wrecker Highway. The problem was we were kind of out in the middle of nowhere. I looked to the left and saw nothing but woods. But the road bent hard to the right and maybe around that corner lay a bank with a nice asphalt parking lot and curbs for board-sliding. I looked to the right and saw nothing but industrial complexes. A whiskey distillery, and some other big confusion of storehouses and smoke stacks and god-knew-what stretched out as far as I could see. All of it fenced against trespassers. But I did notice what looked like a sideroad between the two. Maybe it led to a parking lot for all the employees. I figured I'd give it a try. If it didn't pay off, I could always go the other way, see what was on the other side of the bend. I had all day.

The whiskey distillery was not just a whiskey distillery. That's just what everyone called it. It made rum and gin too. "Rot gut," my dad said. "Poor quality stuff." It sure did smell like hell. Kind of a rotten orange smell. "Oh, you'll get used to it," he said. "I lived out this way when I was in high school, and it got to where you didn't even notice it." The smell was so pungent and intense that I couldn't imagine not smelling it.

I took the road that ran between the distillery and the other place, which turned out to be an orange juice factory. Aunt Twyla, I would find out, worked there, as a shift supervisor on the loading docks. They made concentrate. The road was long and I almost gave out a mile in. Passed the factories a stretch of woods opened up, a buffer, and then, beyond it, a neighborhood. I got a little excited. I picked up the pace. Ditches skirted either side of the road and as you got to the start of the neighborhood the ditch became paved with concrete, and I saw some graffiti—signs of civilization. I stopped and walked over to the ditch on the right. It was grown over with weeds and cracks ran all over it: not much use to anyone. But on the left, it was almost pristine. It looked like someone had been maintaining it, grooming it for use. On the far side of the ditch, along the transition, the words BUTTHOLE BOWL were spray-painted in black. Then I saw an anarchy sign and a Black Flag logo, and a little further down, in red, someone had written Circle Jerks. This was it. I'd found my tribe. I glanced around. Where is everybody on a Saturday afternoon? I thought.

I skated the ditch for about half an hour and then I skated into the neighborhood. Many of the houses were run down and some of them were sloppily painted odd colors, like purple and pink. At first, no one seemed to be out. But once I got a few blocks in I started to see some people. I saw an old man sitting in a lawn chair under a carport. He waved when I pushed by and said something like "Ho," but he didn't smile. Then I came upon an old lady unloading groceries from the trunk of an old car, what I took to be a Cadillac. In fact, all the cars were old, to match the houses. I saw a four- or five-your-old boy in a side yard. He made a "Vrooom!" sound and pushed a toy semi and trailer. Up the road a little ways I saw a large structure, what looked like a school. I'm in luck, I thought. Schools always had some good skateboarding: curbs and rails and stairs and picnic tables and parking lots. I stopped and picked up my board and decided to walk until I got to the school. The road here was bad, anyway, made of pebbles, and not good for skating. Plus I wanted to take my time, take things in. I'd never been in a neighborhood like this, old and kind of rundown and there was just something about it I couldn't quite place. A man, with a pronounced limp, opened up the front door of a mint-green house and stepped out onto the stoop. He nodded at me and smiled. He took a pipe out of his shirt pocket and put it in his mouth. He was a black man. And then it hit me. Every person I'd seen in this neighborhood was black. I was in a black neighborhood. Where I came from there were no black neighborhoods. No white neighborhoods. There were just neighborhoods. I got a little freaked out for a second because I thought maybe I was supposed to be scared. Maybe I didn't belong here. Maybe this was a dangerous neighborhood. But everyone I'd seen had smiled or nodded and I didn't feel in danger.

The school was called Fruit Hollow High School.

Fruit Hollow was a small town next to Summerdale, where our house waited on us. The campus was large. I found the cafeteria and sat down on a wooden bench outside of it. After a few minutes I heard something. Voices, a little ways off. Laughing and yelling, and I heard the unmistakable sound of skateboards clattering and clapping against concrete. I got up and skated towards the sounds.

I got to the other side of the school, where there were racquetball courts, and next to them was a big pavilion with two picnic tables under it. I saw two boys, about my age, sitting on one of the tables talking. I paused and watched. I couldn't tell what they were talking about, but after a few minutes, one of them, a very tall dark-haired boy, gut up and smacked the other one, a medium sized redhead, on the shoulder and took off. The redheaded one said, "All right, man. See you later." He didn't leave, but started skating around in a circle under the pavilion, doing tricks, ollies and shove-its and variels and kickflips, and I even watched him land a heelflip. I decided to go over to him. Once I got about forty feet away, he stopped and squinted at me.

"Hey, there," I said. I popped my board up and walked over to him.

He nodded and popped his board up to, but didn't move.

His board was beat up and he looked a little rough, himself. He had on a baseball cap, backwards, and tore up hightop Airwalks that were bright yellow. He had a ratty Dead Kennedys shirt on, just the band logo, which reminded me of the ditch with the graffiti in it. His hair was deep red and his face was covered in orange freckles.

"I'm Neil," I said.

"Name's Dude." His voice was deep and scratchy. He held out his hand.

"Dude?" I said.

"Yep. Dude."

"I'm new in town. I saw the ditch back there and just kinda been skating around. Getting to know the area. We just moved here a few days ago."

"My apologies."

"Yeah," I looked around. "It's a lot different from where we lived before."

"Where's that?" he said. He pulled a pack of cigarettes out of his short's pocket and lit one up and took a deep, expert drag of it.

"The beach. We lived on the East Coast. Near Cocoa." I knew better than to say the name of my town, which no one had heard of, but most people knew Cocoa.

"Man, that sucks for you. It's nice out there. Where do you live, exactly?"

"For now, just on the other side of that distillery." I pointed in the direction. He nodded. "We're just staying with my aunt and uncle until our place is ready. They live on some land out that way."

"I live about three blocks from here." He threw his cigarette down and stepped on it. "Why don't you ride with me and I'll show you. I gotta head home."

He lived in a decent looking place, a house about the size of the one we'd left to move here. No one was home, so I went in with him and we hung out in his room and listened to music for a little while: *Social Distortion* and *The Misfits*. He looked at his watch and said I'd better be going but I could stop by any time and he'd show me all the good places to skate and he'd introduce me to everybody.

"Everybody?" I said.

"Yeah. Everybody. You'd be surprised at how many of us there are—that skate and listen to cool music and stuff. It won't be all bad for you here." He smiled.

I walked most of the way through the black

neighborhood and a little boy, about eight, followed me. He said, "Hey, Cracker!" I turned and saw him, wearing too-big unlaced hightops, running at me. I stopped and glanced around in alarm. He just wanted to 'try out' my skateboard. I let him get on it and he pushed along with me until we reached the Minute Maid plant.

"I always wanted me one of these things," he said.

"Always?" I said.

"All my life," he said. He hopped off my skateboard and asked me if I had a cigarette.

"How old are you?" I said. I picked up my skateboard.

"Twelve."

"No you ain't."

"How old are you?"

"Fifteen." I lied. I wouldn't be fifteen for a few months.

"No you ain't. Pussy ass white boy."

"You better get the hell out of here before I kick your little ass."

He smiled and took off running so fast he almost tripped a couple of times. He wasn't scared of me. You could tell it was just his habit to move quickly. I got the feeling he did everything full tilt, but I couldn't figure out how he managed to do it in those untied shoes.

Two

WE LEFT THE FARM AND MOVED INTO OUR new home in Summerdale. It was in a shabby residential area about a mile and a half from Dude's, and just barely outside Fruit Hollow city limits, although I didn't realize this at the time. The house was large, bigger than our house at the beach. In our old place we only had a living room. In this new place we had a living room and a family room. When I asked what the difference was, no one seemed to have a strong answer. The best I got was from mom, who said, "Just think of it as two living rooms. We have two living rooms now."

It took a day and a half to fill the house up with all our crap. We had lots of help from family—now that we lived near them. Uncle Corley and Aunt Twyla came. Twyla went for lunch. They loved Church's Chicken. You could get livers and gizzards from Church's. I liked the gizzards a lot and only liked the livers a little. But dipped in hot sauce or gravy anything was good. My uncle Lonny came to help, too. Boy, Uncle Lonny could talk. He always smiled and rubbed his chest and scratched his scalp as he talked, and his eyes would light up and dim down as he told his tales. You got so used to him talking that you learned to listen without giving him total attention. Uncle Lonny was really my first cousin. My dad was his uncle and they looked alike. Lonny was just a little shorter than dad, but dad was heavier. You could tell they really loved each other and they knew everyone thought they looked alike. They were almost like brothers. One day Lonny was standing in one of our new living rooms, holding forth, telling a story about how when he was a kid he'd wait in ditches for black kids to walk by and he'd jump out and scare them and start fights with them. This story mortified me, so I was happy to see my dad walk by and smack him in the head and tell him he was a liar, and couldn't beat the shit out of nobody. My dad didn't like that kind of talk, anyway. Somehow, my dad grew up with these folks and didn't have a racist or bigoted bone in his body. I didn't quite realize it then, but I picked up on it here and there. He couldn't stand to hear the n-word, or any of its proxies.

But all these men and women loved each other dearly. These uncles, aunts and cousins, including my dad, were constantly wrestling, cussing, punching and pranking each other. That's how they showed their love, by inflicting minor pains and annoyances on one another. I loved it. It was fun to watch, and I felt particularly honored when they included me. It wasn't bullying when they noogied you. It wasn't out of meanness when they put you in a headlock or a leglock and Charlie-horsed or frogged you or gave you, god forbid, a wet willie. It was done out of love. If they didn't like you, they'd ignored you. Being ignore by one of them was the worst abuse I could imagine.

Lonny's wife, aunt Maggie, took to giving me wet

willies, as a matter of fact. I'd be standing, enthralled, listening to Lonny or Corley tell a story about hunting or something and I'd be taken by total surprise and disgust to feel a sopping wet pointer inserted in my ear. I'd react and Maggie would let out a squawk of pure delight. Twyla was more reserved, but she'd stand back and watch and giggle and smile at all these crazy people she adored showing their annoying, irritating love for each other.

I was delighted too. I was hooked. These people were great. Those two days of moving into our new place, with our family helping out, asking nothing in return, and doing so playfully and happily, made me realize what we had been missing out on when we had been living away from them. The beach was nice, for sure, but this was better. We'd been kind of alone out there. That wasn't the case here. It seemed like we'd never be alone again. There'd always be someone around to help or pitch in or just hang around with when there was nothing to do. I could see the appeal in this for my dad. I felt like I understood a little bit better why he wanted to move here. He'd missed his family. Maybe it was that simple, maybe it wasn't. All of this familial bonding made me realize another thing too. I'd not been treating my little brother well. I'd been ignoring him, at best, and when I did acknowledge his existence I treated him like shit. I made a vow, that night, to be a better brother. I'd try to treat him more like these men treated each other. They had so many stories about each other, not all of them nice—but still, stories. What did James and I have? I'd try to make more stories with my brother. I'd try to be a better brother to James.

That night I let James stay in my room with me. We made a makeshift tent and stayed up late reading comic books and eating Doritos. It was pretty fun. And when he fell asleep, I exercised extreme self-control. I didn't color his face with markers and I didn't stick anything up his nose. I let him rest, because I knew that I felt like I needed some good rest, and figured he felt the same. It had been a long summer already, and it wasn't even halfway over. We all needed to rest up.

***

I found my way back to Dude's one day, without even realizing it. I turned down a neighborhood street and walked a few houses down and there he was, standing in his yard. The tall, dark-haired boy from the school, that first encounter was there too. They turned, saw me, and Dude smiled and pointed at me. The other boy didn't smile.

"What's up, man?" said Dude.

I nodded and looked at the other guy. He had to be six-two, at least, lanky and sort of limp-limbed.

"This here's Josh," said Dude.

I nodded and put my hand out. He did not take it up.

"I don't like it," he said. "He looks just like Spencer."

Dude looked at me, tilted his head, grimaced.

"Kinda. But not that much."

"No, he looks just goddamn like him. He's even kind of fat like Spencer." He talked about me like I couldn't hear him. I didn't like him.

"You got a problem, man?" I said. I dropped my skateboard, and took a step closer, which made Josh seem even taller. I don't know what I thought I would do. I'd never been in an actual fight, never actually hit anyone before except for that time I'd hit George and he'd laughed at me afterwards.

Josh smiled. "I take it back. He's all right." He and Dude laughed, and Dude called Josh an asshole and Josh put his hand out and we shook hands. "It's cool, man," he said.

"But, dude. You do look like Spencer. You're his goddamn doppelganger."

"What the fuck's that mean?"

"Mean's you're like his mysterious, unrelated twin and shit," said Josh.

I asked who Spencer was, and Dude explained that Spencer had been a core member of their group who, at the end of the school year had to move to Nebraska, to be with his mom. His parents were going through an ugly divorce. Spencer never had a choice. His dad was abusive and even threatened to kill his mom.

"Spencer's dad," Josh explained, "is fucking psycho. He drinks a lot and drives this creepy white van and shit. He doesn't even know where Spencer and his mom went off to. You'll see him every once in a while. If he sees a bunch of kids skating in a parking lot or wherever, he'll drive by real slow and look for Spencer."

"Spencer's pretty fucking crazy, too," added Dude with a smile.

Josh looked over at Dude and he smiled back. "Yes Hell, he is," he added, and they both kind of chuckled.

"Let's go get Cowboy," said Josh, and they jumped on their boards and Dude waved me on with a smile. I took up the rear.

***

After about a mile of weaving through a neighborhood of mismatched houses, we arrived in downtown Fruit Hollow. Downtown wasn't much: a grassy park, called Confederate Park, in the middle of a square of shops and municipal buildings. Just on the other side of downtown was a wide street with about six tiny white houses that looked exactly the same. "Old migrant homes. Shotgun shacks," my dad would later explain. We walked up to one. Josh knocked and I heard the floor creak. The door opened on a dark room and a very fat woman wearing some kind of sheer house gown stepped out. She was in her early forties, I guessed, and once she was in the daylight you could almost see through her gown it was so thin and worn out. She had a little tuft of white hair on her chin too. I'd never seen someone in such a state.

"Hey, Judy," said Josh. "We was wondering if Cowboy was home."

"Was you?" she said in a mocking way. "Why don't you come inside and stay a while."

"Fuck that," said Dude. "Cowboy!" he yelled.

"You can't blame me for trying," said the obese woman. "Who's this?" she said with a nod in my direction.

"He's the new guy," said Josh. "Don't he look like Spencer?"

She took a second to look me over. "Matter of fact, he does. But he's cuter." She walked to the edge of the creaky porch. "Why don't you come inside and keep me company."

Josh laughed, and Dude acted like he was gagging.

"Leave him alone," said Dude. "He don't want nothing to do with an old, fat fartbag like you."

She stuck her tongue out at Dude and quickly lifted up her gown, revealing her completely nude body, full of folds and mounds of impossibly white flesh.

"Oh god! I'm blind!" said Dude, and Josh just laughed some more. I was shocked.

"Robert's over at Louis's you degenerate little shits!" said the woman, and with that we took off.

"Who the hell was that?" I said.

"Cowboy's mom," said Josh.

I couldn't believe that woman was someone's mom.

"She's nasty, ain't she?" said Dude.

I was speechless.

"Louis has fucked her," said Josh as if it was just a simple matter of fact that some teenage kid had had sex with his friend's mom.

"That's disgusting," I said. "That's' terrible." This Louis-guy must be some kind of freak.

They both laughed.

"I let her give me a blowjob!" said Dude.

"What the hell?!" I said.

They both just laughed again.

"We're headed over to Louis' place, and Cowboy thinks it's real funny if you call Louis his daddy, so you should make sure you do that at least once while we're there."

Louis' place consisted of a dilapidated doublewide trailer on a big, shady lot of about two acres. It became evident that his parents weren't around a lot, as the place was very messy and Louis had a too-comfortable-for-regular-adult-supervision air about him. We were there long enough to pick up Cowboy and talk to Louis briefly. Josh introduced me to Louis, who grinned wide, revealing a mouth of the yellowest teeth I'd ever seen, and to Cowboy, who had a thick, blond beard and a mouthful of dip.

"Y'all go on ahead without me. I got a thing with Yolanda," said Louis, with a wink.

"Seriously?" said Dude. He looked over at Josh. Josh grinned and shook his head.

"Who's Yolanda?" I said.

"She's this super hot married gal."

"Married?"

"She's only thirty," said Louis, as if that cleared things up somehow. "I fucked a sixty-five-year-old lady wunst." He cooed out a perverse laugh and scratched his shoulder. To us, who were all in our early teens (except

Louis, who I'd find out later was actually sixteen. He'd been held back a couple times) thirty was pretty damn old, not to mention sixty-five.

"You are my goddamn hero," said Josh. "Honestly." He turned to Cowboy. "All right, then. Kiss your daddy goodbye, so we can get on out of here."

◆

Three

I HAD TO ADMIT THAT THINGS WERE GOING fairly well for me. I'd met some cool people and was really digging in. My parents seemed happy for the most part too. This move, now, seemed like a good thing. I missed some aspects of my old life, back at the beach, but we'd *rolled, baby, rolled,* and this was where we ended up, and that was fine with me.

One day towards the end of summer, a Tuesday I believe, I sat around the house, watching MTV and eating Little Debbie oatmeal cream pies, and James came in from outside and ran straight to his room. This was unusual because, ordinarily, if I was home, and he came in he'd come by and irritate me. This was not his usual behavior. He's hiding something, I thought, and got up and walked down the hallway to his room. The door was closed. I banged on it.

"Open the door, shithead."

He didn't answer, but I heard him sniffling.

"If you don't open the door, I'm gonna kick your ass when you finally do come out."

No answer, but I could hear him walking towards the door. He opened the door and I could tell he'd been crying.

"What the hell's your problem?"

"Just leave me alone."

"Why were you crying?" For some reason I couldn't quite figure out, I was getting a little jittery. I sensed a wrong had been done to him. I did what any big bro would do—I, again, threatened my little brother with violence if he did not tell me what was going on.

"Jesus! Okay," he said. "Everyone around here wants to beat me up or something—even you." He glanced at me with big, sad, brown little brother eyes, and I got even more jittery.

And he hit me with it.

See, there was this kid, named Duper, who lived down the street and I'd already suspected that he'd taken to picking on James. I'd let it slide so far, because it was mostly harmless stuff he did to him, and a lot of times it was pretty funny. For instance, one time he dared James to get in his pool naked. When James did, Duper took his clothes. James had to run home—only three houses down—covering his privates and crying the whole way. That's funny. I had to applaud him for that one. But it looked like this time he'd crossed a line. James had come home crying, not just embarrassed or pissed off, but crying.

This Duper kid had, it turned out, spit in my little bro's face, and he'd done it in front of a little girl he knew James liked. Put aside the fact that the little girl was about five levels beyond James' station, this was a major league infraction in my book. Also, if you're the kind of dude that spits in the face of a little kid, you're just a piece of dog shit.

According to James it had been a big ole goober gob of spit too. Hit him right in the eye with it. And that little girl, Lulabelle or whoever, had laughed right in his face. I was pissed.

"Come on," I said.

"What?"

"You think he's still out there?"

"I don't know. What are you gonna do?"

"Pay him back, that's what."

And right then I realized what it was that got me about this. Sure, I was pissed because some asshole had done something cruel to my little bro, but on another level, it was personal. It made me think of the goddamn Nooch, my own personal bully. We'd moved, but all that he'd done to me had moved with us. It was like he was still bullying me. It seemed like, maybe, getting back at James' bully would make me feel better about everything.

***

We walked out to the edge of our driveway. The sun was low but it was hot and humid and bright. I'd been in the house all day and it took some time for my eyes to adjust.

"There he is," whispered James. He was standing at the edge of his driveway, shooting hoops. That little girl was still down there too. She and Duper's little brother, Andy, sat in a couple of these bright red Little Tike chairs. She was combing a Barbie doll's hair and Andy was picking his nose watching his big brother miss layups.

When Duper noticed us standing at the end of his driveway he stopped and smiled. His little brother pulled his finger out of his nose and stuck his hand under the plastic chair and then placed it in his lap. The girl ignored us.

"You spit on James?" I figured I'd get straight to it.

He took a step back, dribbled the basketball, took a shot, and missed. His little brother watched. Duper caught the rebounded ball and turned back to us, ball on his side, held in place by his forearm.

"Yeah. So?"

I had to admit, even though I was older than Duper, he was my size, and a bit more athletic looking. I couldn't fault him for not seeing me as a threat, but I had purpose and felt emboldened by it.

"I saw the whole thing," said the little girl, not looking up from combing her dolls hair.

"Take her clothes off. Does she have girl parts?" Andy motioned towards the doll and the little girl moved the doll away from him.

"You're disgusting."

"That your little brother," I said.

"Yeah, so?" said Duper.

"Those the only two words you know?"

James was still right next to me, not moving, not saying a word.

"I know a couple more," said Duper. He stepped back and dribbled the ball some more.

I walked into the yard, stood next to his little brother, and stopped. He stopped dribbling. I put the palm of my hand on his brother's forehead and pushed. He fell back and landed on a cushion of grass with a soft thud. He whined a little, but clearly was not hurt. James tugged on my shirt, as if to say, come on, let's go home. Duper threw the ball down and walked up to me, completely ignoring his brother. He got right in my face. I cleared my throat, got a good gob worked up, and spit it right in Duper's face. I braced myself for an attack, but there was nothing. He flinched and took a few steps back. Andy ran up to him and grabbed his brother's hand, crying harder now. To my surprise, Duper was crying now.

"You…bully," said Andy. They both turned and went inside. The little girl put her doll in a pocket she had on the front of dress, facing out, like she was giving her a ride.

"He deserved it," she said and took off running down the street.

"We better head home before their parents come outside," said James.

I took up his hand and we turned and took our time walking home.

***

Summer was almost over now and I was nervous about school. I'd be in high school, the ninth grade, and, if that wasn't enough, I'd be at a different school, one where I knew only a handful of people. I'd met about twelve people by now, and knew eight of them fairly well. They were all pretty cool and things were going well, but all I knew about the social situation once school started was stuff these eight pretty unreliable skate-punk kids told me. And they *were* punks. I could tell that *easily* at least fifty percent of what they said was total bullshit, played for effect, just to freak me out. Dude was straightforward, didn't go in for a lot of embellishment, so I trusted him the most. Cowboy was as good as mute on just about any subject, except for skateboarding, about which he could be almost poetic. Josh was home-schooled, so he wasn't a bunch of help. That left Ira, Mike and Mitch. Mitch was probably the worst, talking about school race riots and teachers who were key members of the KKK. Ira and Mike told mostly straight stories with a little flourish here and there. But it was easy to tell when they were screwing with me, because eyes would widen and voices would lower to almost a whisper and everything took on this mythic quality. Ira told one story about this hick kid, named Reginald Suderland, that seemed to me like a real hatchet job—lots of hushed tones and eye-widening. Apparently, he was six-foot-seven and twenty-three years old.

"The dude will finally be in the twelfth grade this year. He was in my sister's English class last year. Wears this massive cowboy hat with a raccoon dick-bone on the front of it. He's pretty cool, actually. He likes to play pool and his dad's this big-time citrus farmer. But here's the thing you won't believe: he's married."

"He's in high school, twenty-three, and he's married?"

Ira leaned back in his chair and held his hand out towards Mitch. "Ain't that right?"

"It's true. His wife's name's Delila, and she's pregnant."

"Why hasn't he dropped out of school?"

"He can't. If he does his dad won't give him the family farm when he retires or whatever. They're rich. Millionaire citrus planters."

"That's just unbelievable. Where I come from shit like that just doesn't happen."

"Welcome to our world," said Ira, smiling. "You're in the country now." Ira stood up and stretched and adjusted his thick glasses. "Your mom buy groceries lately, Mitch?" Ira, I'd learned, was always hungry. He walked into the kitchen and we all got up and followed. Ira was like me, an outsider, but he'd been around longer. He was going into the tenth grade, and had lived in the area since the sixth grade. His father was a bank president or something and they'd moved around kind of a lot. He stood out for two reasons. One, his family had money and they lived in the only 'rich people'' neighborhood in town, a gated subdivision, a place called Cypress Greens. Two, he was Jewish. They weren't practicing Jews, but it was still a strange thing for Lawrence County. The only Jewish family around, as far as anyone knew. But none of that mattered to us. He was cool and fun to be around. That was the main thing.

***

The Saturday before school would start Dad and Uncle Corley took me and James and Will to an old phosphate mine that was now used as a swimming hole. A huge live oak stood next to it that someone years ago had tied a rope swing to. There were phosphate mines all over Lawrence county and people had been swimming in them for years.

"Before they started mining out here there was a big to-do about it," said Corley. "The mining industry had to pay the state government a bunch of money. It was supposed to be a national park, but it never did happen that way."

"What's so special about it out here?" said Will.

"It's special in a lot of ways. Ponce de Leon came through here in his travels, on his fabled search for the fountain of youth, some say. Over the years people've found all kind of shit out here, too, pre-Seminole Indians shit, and at one time they was a Indian village out here."

I stood on the edge of the cliff-like side of the mine and looked into the water, Indians and conquistadores circling through my thoughts, fighting each other and trading with each other, and smoking tobacco together. I had just about worked up the nerve to grab hold of the rope swing and go for it.

"But that ain't my favorite reason why this here's a special place." Corley took off his shirt and stretched. Dad lit a cigarette and started heeling his shoes off. Corley winked at dad.

"What is it, then?" said Will.

"Go ahead and take hold of that rope and swing on in, I'll tell ya. We need someone to christen that bad boy."

Will did as his dad said. He took hold of it and ran and swung out and let go once the rope swung as far as it would go. He said "WOOOOO!!!" and smacked against the clear blue water.

"That sounded like it hurt," said Corley.

"Your turn," said dad.

"You ain't scared, are ya?" said Corley.

"Hell no." I grabbed the rope and did like Will, but I went in feet first like a knife and went several feet under and could feel the water drop in temperature as I plunged. When I emerged Corley and Dad were jumping off without the use of the rope.

We all treaded water, heads bobbing up and down in the wake of their jumping.

"Well," said Will. "What was your other, most favorite special thing about this place?"

"It's the only place in the world, as far as anybody knows, where rattlesnakes and water moccasins interbreed."

"What the hell!" said Will.

"That's the scariest, most disgusting thing I've ever heard," I said. "That's like a mythological beast or something. Je-sus…"

"It's called a super-rattler. They're very aggressive and grow to twice the size of a moccasin or a rattler. Been known to climb into trees and wait for prey to walk under and then drop out onto it."

Right then Dad said, "SHHHHH!"

We all got quiet. I was about to shit myself with fear. I imagined a horde of super-rattlers winding their way up from the deep, all of them going straight for my legs.

"What?" said Will.

"Thought I heard something off in that grass over

there."

"I heard it too," said Corley.

"Y'all are just messing with us," said Will.

"No hell I ain't," said Corley. "I heard something."

"I'm getting the hell out of here!" Will started to swim toward the steps carved in the side of the mine that led up to where the swing was.

"Stop right there," said Dad. "They're attracted to movement, so I'd advise against swimming in that direction."

"What do I do?" he whispered. "I'm about to lose my mind!" He turned and his eyes were widened and his mouth contorted.

"Quit playing, Dad," I said. "I'm getting scared too." I just kept doggy paddling and trying to keep my cool, both of which were increasingly hard to do.

We were all looking in the direction of Will and we all noticed a snake, head a few inches out of the water, swerving its way towards him. Will was the only one who didn't know. I said nothing, just waited for Corley or Dad to say something. The snake veered off to the right and disappeared into some weeds.

"You know what," said Corley. "You go on ahead, son. We were just pulling your leg." That's when I knew Corley was scared too, and that's when I lost it. I swam over to my dad and, just like a goddamn toddler, grabbed him around the neck and put my legs around his torso. I was about to cry.

"Come on, now," said dad. "Everything's fine. Just follow Will. Look, he's already out." I saw that he was, but still couldn't move.

Will stood on the edge of the cliff. "Goddamn! You assholes scared the shit out of me." He was doubled over laughing now. His attitude about the whole thing lightened my mood and I let go of my dad, but still couldn't bring myself to start swimming in the direction I'd seen the snake in.

"I'll go first," said Dad. He started, slowly, doing a kind of freestyle breaststroke. He got about six feet away from me and started screaming, "Oh, shit! Oh shit! No!" At that I lost hold of all reason and just took off, but in the opposite direction, to the other side of the phosphate mine where I'd noticed there was a little platform of rock about two feet out of the water.

They were all out of the water and standing by the rope swing staring at me on the other side standing on the flat rock. I was a good twenty to thirty yards away from them and there was no way for them to come get me. I knew it— I'd have to get back in the water and swim across to where they were. It wasn't that big a deal. I did it. But you can bet that once I got about halfway, they all started screaming snake and pointing and scared me so bad I got a cramp in my calf from swimming so hard.

***

Sitting in Corley's pickup on the way home all I could think about at first was monster water snakes and how close we'd come to some real trouble. I still had some of that fear in me. But then I started to think about next Monday and having to go to a new school—a high school, no less—and super rattlers didn't seem all that bad compared to a whole high school of strangers.

Four

DAD COMMUTED TO THE BEACH FOR WORK, A two-hour drive, so he got me up for school. He worked twenty-four hour shifts every other day and got up about an hour before me. He would wake me up on his way out. I would wake up and then fall back to sleep, so my dad had to make sure I was really awake before he left. Extreme tactics were sometimes in order, but not this morning. It was my first day at a new school and my first day of high school. I was wide awake, wired and hadn't slept much. When dad came into my room and uttered his, "Get up, boy!" I was just lying there in bed staring at the ceiling imagining first-day scenarios. "I'm up, Dad," I said.

"I'm gonna need you to get *out* of bed."

I had a piece of buttered toast for breakfast and horked it down. I grabbed my skateboard and took off for school: it was about two-and-a-half miles of mostly good asphalt. I'd scoped it out beforehand, so I'd already know a good route once school started. There was one section of it, about halfway in, where the neighborhood stopped and gave way to rural farmland and then went back to houses again, a strange, anomalous half-mile or so of hard-packed dirt road that cut through a cow pasture, fenced in with barbwire. This strange geographical shift didn't bother me. I liked it. I developed an odd, reverent manner when walking through it, slow and quiet, and sometimes I'd stop and watch the cows mingle about. I didn't see one person, not one. It almost seemed like my own place, a redneck-ass Narnia or something that only I could see.

As I got close to school, before I could even see it, I could hear voices—laughing, screaming, talking loud. I looked at my watch. I had plenty of time. I got off my board and crept slowly. I took a corner and saw the south end of the school, the dead end of a covered hallway that led to the cafeteria. A horde of kids stood, milling around. I approached and felt my body go frail with fear and anticipation. But no one had stopped to laugh and point at me. So far, so good. And just when I had the urge to turn and head back the way I came, I heard a familiar voice, "Neil! Over here, man!" and before I even saw where the voice was coming from I felt relieved. Dude came walking out of the horde, skateboard in hand, smiling. I could see that the right side of the horde was our side. It was the freak side. Behind Dude was a whole group of skaters, punks, new-wave chicks and metalheads, a good thirty deep. This was a relief, as well. We had numbers.

"You probably need to go to the office, since it's your first day. You want me to take you?"

I nodded. A guy with a green Mohawk came up behind Dude. He was wearing a GBH shirt and tattered blue jeans.

"Who's this?"

"Neil," said Dude. "This is Corey."

We gave each other cool-guy nods. Dude and I walked into the heart of the horde. As we walked by our group to get through to the other side, I noticed a fair bevy of girls, maybe eight or ten, which was heartening. I wondered how many were unfettered. I got to thinking about how here, in Bum Fuck Egypt, ninth grade was high school, and sixth through eighth was called middle school. So weird. Back at the beach we had junior high—seventh, eighth and ninth—and high school was tenth through twelfth. Why the difference? I didn't know, but I liked it this way. For me, it had a symmetry to it. Here, I was a new guy, but I was starting a new grade at a new school along with everyone else, so we were all a little awkward together. Before we got to the end of the covered walk where the front office was, I saw something off in the distance. Out by the football field, walking in a field, was maybe the tallest person I'd ever seen. He walked up a berm, behind which was a huge fenced-in parking lot, so he was bent forward a little. He wore a big black cowboy hat and a plaid button up shirt and tight black jeans.

"Who's that?" I said to Dude.

"That's Reginald Suderland, man."

"Holy shit! He's real…"

"We told you."

The tall man-boy passed in front of us.

"Hey, Reginald," said Dude, and the freakishy tall figure lifted his hat, just like some TV cowboy, and dropped it quickly back onto his head.

***

It turned out that all the girls but one in my new clique were already spoken for. A poor old gal who went by the name Mudfish. Any time I asked why she was called that all anyone would do was laugh and say something like, "You'll find out," or, "I'll tell you later." Even some of the other girls called her Mudfish, instead of her name, which was Teresa. I couldn't figure it out. She was actually kind of cute. She was a little on the heavy side, but not by much and, despite running with a group of people who called her Mudfish, she was exceedingly friendly. Even Dude, who by now had essentially become my best friend, didn't want to tell me why Teresa was called Mudfish. I figured I'd steer clear of developing too fast a friendship with her until I found out why she had such a peculiar nickname.

The first day was not too bad, and by week two things were humming along. I even had a few of my new friends in some of my classes. Dude was in my PE class, and he was in Biology with me and Josh. Corey, the Mohawk guy, was in my JROTC class. I only took the JROTC class because I had somehow been signed up for it and now had to stay in until the end of the semester. Mike, who apparently was as bad at math as me, was in my Consumer Math class. Ira was in Art with me, along with this girl named Louise, who wasn't really a part of any group, but was a kind of hybrid Metalhead-Brain-Freak. Her chestnut hair, all one length, was so long it framed her ass, and she wore tight jeans and a denim jacket with patches all over it of obscure metal, thrash and punk bands. She smoked filterless Camels. She was a tough nut to crack. I liked her right away.

After art one day during the second week of school, I said something to Ira about her.

"What you like her, or something?" Ira asked.

"I mean, she seems cool," I said.

He shook his head.

"What?"

"I don't know her that well, but I'd stay away from her."

"Why?" I said.

"She's supposed to be kind of a nutcase—damaged goods. I've heard her dad abuses her and shit."

"Abuses?"

"Yes. Like hits her and locks her in her room. Stuff like that. That's why she's kind of dark and quiet."

"How do you know all this?"

"It's just common knowledge. Everyone knows. Ask anyone."

I let it go. I didn't know about any of that other stuff—but I decided to keep it on the down-low. You couldn't get too obvious about things like this. Liking a girl, and professing that you did, was a kind of tightrope walk. You had to do it with a kind of nonchalance that I had not learned to master yet. You had to pretend you didn't really care, one way or the other, if she liked you back or not. You had to get real laidback about shit, even though you were all electricity on the inside. Adolescence is all about these kinds of hard to negotiate incongruities. Most teenagers are bad actors.

But not Dude. Dude just flat didn't give a shit about anything or anyone—or so it seemed. His confidence was inspiring. When you were around Dude you acted like Dude. This happened to everyone, though none of us admitted it. And it wasn't that he was king stud or anything. He just acted like he was, and acting that way kind of made it true. Plenty of boys were taller, better looking, better skaters, whiter teeth, dated prettier girls, but even a lot of those guys looked up to Dude. Plus he had a voice like that Frog kid on *The Little Rascals*, and he smoked Marlboro Reds. He just had a way about him that got to you, made you want to be more like him and less like yourself.

One day, well into freshman year, Dude and I were walking down the hall from the lunchroom to class and a big jock, a senior football player, came up from behind us and flipped Dude's hat off (he always wore a Braves baseball cap backwards). Dude stopped, bent down and picked the hat off the ground and slowly put it back on. He stood tall and walked over to the football player, got to where his nose was almost touching the football player's nose and stood there. The football player chuckled, tried to laugh it off. One of his buddies was standing next to him, a somewhat shorter guy, who was built like a badger. He reached up towards Dude's hat and Dude smacked his hand away, while still locking eyes with the first guy. Both did nothing. It was like Dude had them hypnotized. They did nothing. Dude quickly made like he was going to punch the first guy but stopped with his fist next to the guy's face. The guy flinched. Dude smiled, and in his Frog voice, said, "Two for flinching, Jock Itch." He then hit the guy twice in the shoulder and walked off. His brazen attitude was legend. He acted like he had nothing to lose, and to teenage boys, that's intimidating as hell. It made us respect him.

As we walked away, Dude turned to me and said, "That went better than expected." I couldn't argue with that.

***

One day in art class, while Ira was home with the flu or diarrhea or some shit, I worked up the nerve to talk to Louise. Art class—this art class—was an easy-going affair. The teacher, Mrs. LeFleur, would give an assignment and then walk around the class, encouraging her students to work and mingle and compare their work. This day we worked on linoleum cuts. For some reason, I had dug the primitive image of a rat into mine. It was basic looking but, I thought, passible as a work of art. I walked over to Louise's table, rat print in hand. She was huddled over her creation, her long hair draped over the table, obscuring what she worked on.

"I don't know," I said. "You seem pretty artistic to me. What do you think?"

She stopped her working and looked over at my rat. She put down her tool and picked up my square piece of linoleum and held it close to her eyes.

"Is it a possum?" she said.

It did look like a possum. Sonofabitch. "Yeah," I said. "It's a possum."

"Why?" She picked it up again. "Why a possum?"

"It's not a possum," I said, snatching it out of her hand. "It's a goddamn rat."

"Oh, good," she said.

I noticed a *Misfits* patch on the shoulder of her denim jacket.

"You like *The Misfits*?"

She blinked at me.

"Of course you do. Why else would you have a patch."

"Not too many people around here know who they are."

"I'm not from around here," I said.

"Where are you from?"

"East coast. The beach."

"Whereabouts, exactly? One of my best friends lives in Palm Bay."

"I know where Palm Bay is. That's not far from Radar Beach, where I'm from."

"Oh, I've heard of that place. Total beach bum town, right?"

"Yeah, military families and beach bum types. That pretty much covers it."

"So you hang around the same crown as Ira, I guess."

"I guess. I'm the new guy, so I barely have a crowd, but yeah."

She smiled and nodded. The bell rang, so it was time to move on. I didn't know what else to say or do so I just walked back to my desk and started to gather up my things. I put my rat print in my portfolio and put my portfolio in the vertical file where Mrs. LeFluer made us keep them all in alphabetical order and when I walked back to my desk I opened my art class folder and found inside of it a piece of scratch paper with the name "Louise" on it and a phone number. Under the number she'd written, "Call me, if you want to."

Five

ONE FRIDAY, AFTER SCHOOL, MY PARENTS had an oyster roast in our backyard. I came home from school and no one was in the house. I heard music coming from the backyard. It was Bob Marley. I went to my room and put my school gear away and changed into shorts and flops, then went out back.

My dad was sitting at a picnic table, a cigarette dangling from his lips, and a portable stereo in front of him. He was shuffling through some CDs. Multicolored Christmas lights were wrapped around the huge juniper bushes in the back corners of the yard, and the big grapefruit tree had some paper lanterns hung in it. Seeing this festive scene brightened my mood.

"What's up, bud?" said my dad when he noticed me walking toward him at the picnic table. He took hold of his cigarette, dragged on it, and put it down on the edge of the picnic table with the cherry hanging off.

"Nothing much," I said. I noticed our Rottweiler, Bomber, was at dad's feet, alert and contented to be next to his favorite person in the world. We'd had him about a month now and the entire household had already cliqued up. There was Bomber's group and then there was me. Tongue out, he blinked at me, and then licked his lips and chomped once, as if in anticipation of a snack. Bomber was dad's dog, not mine or James's, and definitely not mom's. But I was the only one he flat out didn't like. I couldn't blame him. I didn't like him either. A man dad worked with had a Rottweiler that had puppies and Bomber had been the runt. Dad had a rule about always taking the runt. "They make the best pets," he said. The dog never fully took to anyone else. My mom fed it, but Bomber didn't give a shit. He liked my dad, tolerated everyone else, and hated me. He wasn't aggressive towards me. But he'd perk up and stop whatever he was doing whenever I was around. He'd just watch me until I left his area. This was okay with me. I'm not a dog person, and never have been, so Bomber was more of a nuisance to me than anything else. I'm sure the feeling was mutual.

"I hope you're in the mood for some oysters," Dad said. He got up and walked to the grill and pulled it over to the picnic table. "Do me a favor and go get the charcoal over there," Dad said pointing at the bag leaned against the house.

I walked over to it, Bomber followed, and picked it up and whipped it over my shoulder and walked it over.

"Put the whole bag on the grill. You just light the whole bag." Dad lit a cigarette with a match. I laid the bag into the belly of the grill and he took the match and touched the flame to the corner and the flame slowly grew until it engulfed the bag. I watched and thought about the fact that my dad was a firefighter. It seemed to mean that he was an expert on matters such as these. He understood fire in ways that everyone else didn't. I looked over at him. I'd always felt proud of him, of him being a firefighter.

He walked to a red and white cooler on the other side of the picnic table and opened it and took out two beers.

"Want a beer?" He held a brown bottle out in my direction.

"Uh, sure," I said. I walked over and took it from him. I tried to open it but couldn't.

"It's a twist-off. If you can't open it yourself you can't drink it."

I took up my shirtfront and tried again. The cap made a sound, a "chit," and it came off. I threw the cap in the charcoal fire and took a sip. It was not my first taste of beer, but it was the first time my dad had offered me a whole beer.

"Don't tell your mom," he said. He took a pull of his beer and drank about half of it.

A tennis ball came flying past me, from behind me, and Bomber went after it. I turned and saw James walking up to where dad and I stood drinking our beers. Bomber brought the ball to our dad and he threw it at the grapefruit tree.

"Are you drinking a beer?"

I didn't answer, but, instead, took a sip of it.

"You want one too?"

James smiled. "No way!"

"Why not?" I said.

"Mom would get mad."

At the exact same time, dad and I said, "Mom's not here."

We laughed and James shook his head and walked up to Bomber and took the slobbery ball and threw it.

***

Two hours later things hummed along and the atmosphere in our backyard was party-like. People were drinking and not drinking and there was about the whole moment a quickness, an unpredictability. I sat at the picnic table and watched, as had become my habit. I'd become a spectator. And I was beginning to see myself as one, as a watcher. I didn't like it. I wanted to be a doer. But when things got going, when lots of people were involved, it was my default. I'd automatically fall back and watch. Being buzzed didn't help.

I saw my aunt Belinda peek around the corner of the house and then waddle into the back yard carrying a case of Busch Lite. She huffed her way towards my father at the grill behind the steaming oysters. When she was halfway there he turned and noticed her, "Bell!" he yelled and her face lit up. They were each other's favorite. Of my father's three sisters she was the kindest, and she'd essentially raised my father. I thought of her as a grandmother more than an aunt. She and her husband lived a few miles away now, so she was the only true aunt I ever saw on anything like a regular basis.

Patricia, the oldest of my dad's sisters, had died before I was born and Aunt Judy was somewhat distant with me. According to my dad, Judy had always been distant with him, so it made sense that she would be with James and me, as well. It wasn't that she treated us badly; she mostly ignored us. Pat's death had been a kind of shake out, a sorting out. As my dad tells it, Pat had been his dad's favorite. His dad was almost never around, but when he was he tended to ignore everyone but Pat and him—therefore Judy, who my dad guessed loved their absent father more than any of the others did, took it hard when Pat died and their father quit coming around. According to my dad, Judy would find reasons to beat him. But he never seemed self-pitying about this when he told it. He told the stories as if they were things that happened to a boy he'd known.

Bell was on her third husband, a man named Paul, who was decades younger than she. This would be my first true introduction to Paul.

"Where's that young feller of yours?" asked Dad.

"He's coming."

Dad peeked past Belinda, looking.

"He's got something."

Just then a young man wearing a backwards trucker's cap and blue jeans, and nothing else, came around the corner with a softshell turtle under his arm and a handgun of some kind tucked into the top of his jeans. He had a big grin on his face.

He approached Belinda and dad and she handed him an opened beer and he took a long drink of it and then sat it on the picnic table. He looked over at me and saw me watching. He winked. The feet of the turtle under his arm swam through the air.

"Hey there, boy!" he said. My dad and aunt looked at me. They knew I didn't like being the center of attention, never have, but I was about to be.

"Hey," I said, barely audibly, and raised a hand.

He dropped the turtle and it scampered off towards the back of the yard and when it reached the wooden fence it started to scratch at it. He put his hand out towards me.

"Name's Paul, young man."

I shook his hand. "Neil."

"I knowed that." He pointed his chin towards the turtle. "You mind going and getting *la tortuga* for me?"

I pointed at my chest.

"Yeah, man."

And what was *la tortuga*?

"The turtle, boy."

I'd never touched a turtle before and the thought of doing so made me feel sick and frightened. What if it scratched me or bit me? What if it was too heavy for me to adroitly handle?

"If you don't want to then don't worry about it," he said. "He ain't going nowhere."

I did not respond, but I walked over to the beast and as I got close it retreated into its shell. I picked it up and carried it over, holding it like it was a too-full bowl of cereal. Paul laughed and took it from me.

"What you gonna do with it?" asked Belinda.

"I figured we'd have some turtle soup. You know how to make turtle soup, right, Bell?"

"I've made it wunst or twiced."

He laid the turtle down on the ground and put his foot on the shell. He took the handgun out of his pants and stuck it in the front of the shell. The turtle bit the nose of the gun and Paul, who I was just realizing was my uncle now, pulled gently on the gun and the turtle, still clamped down on the nose of it, came out. He did this until the neck looked like it was two feet long or more.

Without warning he pulled the trigger of the gun. Everyone stopped still and looked his way. Still holding the gun in one hand he picked the turtle up by the bloody head and held it up. Just then my mom walked out of the house and saw what was going on.

"Belinda… Paul," she said.

Paul took a buck knife out of a belt holster and cut the turtle's neck at the shell and handed the neck and head to Belinda.

"Y'all take that inside and get some soup going."

Belinda took it and a fresh beer and waddled over to my mom, who had a grimace on her face and they both went inside.

Paul held the gun up to his eyes.

"Look here," he said. "Bite marks clean into the

barrel."

And there were. The turtle had bitten a line into the gun metal.

***

After a while it started to rain and we all straightened up the backyard and headed inside. I could smell something cooking, the turtle, and went into the kitchen where my mom and Belinda were laughing and talking, a big pot on the stove top.

"So this is turtle soup, huh?'

I picked up the long-handled wooden spoon and spooned out some broth and took a cautious sip. It was good, oily and salty and mild. The wind and rain picked up outside. Dad turned on the TV, news of the tropical storm approaching. The weatherman said that it could strengthen to a category one or two before hitting central Florida, our part of Florida. I found this news exciting. My beer buzz had worn off and I felt tired.

I sat on the back living room couch and replayed the grizzly scene that had taken place in our backyard. I felt sick about the turtle, but not sick enough to be bothered. People, I thought, had been killing turtles for thousands of years—maybe a hundred-thousand years, maybe more. How long had there been people? I vaguely thought. But the way Paul, my too-young new uncle, had done it seemed almost disrespectful. I could almost be a vegetarian, I thought. Too bad meat tasted so good. Just then the wind gusted up and something bounced off the back of the house. Paul let out a loud "WOOO!" and Bellinda yelled, "soup's done."

***

The storm had been downgraded from a category one to a tropical depression. It exploded into bands and bursts and showered central Florida with a steady curtain of rain for the better part of a week. Ira and Dude and I made plans for the following weekend, which included a possible party at a friend of Dude's older brother, a guy who'd graduated from our high school two years ago and had an apartment in town. None of us had been to a proper party before. That is, we'd never seen the likes of the types of parties one saw in movies and on TV. This party seemed to us like it could be a first for us. A big crowd was supposed to show up, and there'd be lots of girls, high school aged and older. Also, Dude said his brother and the guy who owned the apartment, a guy named Karl, were getting a keg. An actual keg. I'd never seen one of those before, not up close and in real life.

In art class, things with Louise were picking up, not dramatically, but enough that we'd developed something— not something you could label, but close to it. I wasn't much of a phone person, but I'd called her a few times. She got my stupid jokes, or pretended to—I didn't care which—and pretty soon we were at the same table. The art teacher, Mrs. LeFleur, did not assign seats.

Because of the constant rain fall and the normal heat and humidity of a typical central Florida summer, it was so muggy out that it was exceedingly uncomfortable. The air was thick and wet and as soon as you stepped outside in the morning you were sweating. By the time I got to school Friday I was soaked through with sweat. But I wasn't the only one. We all suffered through the same condition. That's the thing about weather, I thought, as I approached my locker. No one is above it. But some of us were better at dealing with it—or better equipped to deal with it.

Ira's locker was three down from mine. He got to his about the same time.

"What's up, sucka!" He slapped me on the back as he walked by.

I got what I needed from my locker and walked over to Ira. He took his shirt off.

"What are you doing?"

He just looked at me as he pulled a fresh shirt from his locker, put it on, and took the sweat-soaked one and sort of hung it up on the bookbag hooks in his locker.

"Okay, smart," I said.

He smiled.

"Hey, you hear anything from Dude about the party?"

"Two people. His bro said he could bring two people."

"Me and you," I said, and winked.

He smiled and winked back.

***

In art class I decided to ask Louise if she wanted to go to the party with me. I wasn't supposed to bring anyone. But I figured I'd give it a shot and if she said yes I'd figure out a way to bring here. I'd never asked a girl out before. Since we sat at the same table now, it made things easier. We were working on self-portraits, and I sidled up to her and took a long look of hers. It was dark, full of blacks and drab greens and browns. Everything was full of detail except her face. The face, the whole head really, was black.

"Interesting," I said. "Where's your face."

"I haven't started the face yet. That's the hardest part. Let's see yours."

I held mine up next to hers. Mine was my best attempt at a realistic portrait—not very creative—just my trying to render myself as best I could. I had done a sketch of everything and had been frantically and somewhat randomly filling parts in. The hair was there in ridiculously defined detail and the eyes. Eyes were my favorite things to draw on a face. But the nose was just two holes in the middle of the face and the lips were a short horizontal line with two hyphen-sized vertical lines on either side.

She looked, and said, "Hunh…"

"I know," I said. "It sucks."

"No. It doesn't suck." She put her index finger on her pursed lips. "It's… promising."

I set my painting down.

"I've been invited to a party this weekend. Some dude named Karl or something. I don't know.

"Yeah?" She put a mark on her picture.

"Yeah… You can come if you want. I mean, I can bring you."

She picked up my picture and lightly filled in the nose. And she did a good job. It was a far better nose than I could ever do. I had eyes down. But noses were tough.

"I've already been invited." She kept working on the nose.

Oh," I said. I gently took my picture away from her.

"My sister. She's going. I guess I shouldn't say invited. My parents told her she couldn't go unless she brought me."

"That's cool, I guess. Are you gonna go?"

"Maybe. Will I see you there if I go?"

"Yeah, I'll see you there."

"Noses are the hardest facial feature to draw."

"They are."

"You're good at eyes. Those are hard too."

Six

I ONLY PARTLY APPRECIATED THAT THIS COUNTY was Dad Country. My father, who had grown up essentially fatherless, but with hordes of family around him, grew up in these environs. And he liked to do what no longer can be innocently done. That is, drive backroads and drink beer. The specter of some death to come is always dangling over your head—or of some death to be caused. One doesn't drink while driving anymore. It's a lost art, and my father was one of its chiefest practitioners. My father drove the backroads of central Florida by feel. His sense of direction was uncanny. Add to that the familiarity of a man who, as a boy, had been on each and every road a hundred times.

"Wanna go for a ride?" my Dad would say, and I never said no, or at least, I cannot remember ever saying no. We didn't say much on these trips but there was an air and feel of camaraderie that I found intoxicating.

We'd stop at a "Six Pack-a-Stani" and get a twelve pack of Busch Lite, maybe a bag of pistachios and some scratch-offs, and ride out.

**

At this point in time, My dad had a late-sixties Ford F-100 that we'd brush-painted beige with a thick satin house paint. You could even find a brush hair in the paint in places. He didn't give a shit. He thought it was funny. Being a ninth grader I looked on it with a twinge of embarrassment, but not while I was with my dad. When I was with him I adopted the same perverse pride he had of it; a kind of *ain't this dumb but ingenious all at once* kind of attitude.

We hopped in the Ford, drove to the store, got the beer, and drove straight out of town and hit an area of lemon groves. It was late afternoon and the sky, just above the horizon, was a tied-eye painting of pinks and grays and purples and blues. "Sky looks Japanese," said dad, who'd never been to Japan, but I knew what he meant, and he was right.

"Have a beer," he said, pointing towards the pack of cans.

I looked at him.

"They're light. It'll be fine."

He took a long, narrow potholed road that decayed into a rutted dirt road with deep ditches on either side. Dad slowed and became more alert. We rode for slow quiet minutes and then he rolled to a stop and looked off to the right.

"Yeah," he whispered. "I think that's it...." He pointed. "See there?"

I saw nothing but woods, thick with trees—mostly scrub oaks and longleaf pines—and underbrush and palmettoes.

"Look up, towards the top of the trees."

"What am I looking for?"

He sighed and when he did I finally saw it jump out at me, and I could hardly believe I hadn't seen it before. It was the tip of a high-gabled roof just peeking out of the top of the woods, almost like a church steeple.

"There's a house back there?"

"Yap."

Dad lit a cigarette and took a swig of his beer.

"Can we go back there? I'd like to see it. I popped open the car door.

"No, we'd better not. Snakes and shit all through there. Plus there are a couple more roads I wanna hit before we head back."

"How old is that house?"

"I don't know…hundred years, maybe more."

"Who lived there?"

"When I was a kid a boy named Randall Vance lived there with his grandparents. The Vances were the richest people around at that time."

"Did you know Randall Vance?"

"Yap. Used to play with him. We were friends until about seventh grade. He became an asshole, got stuck up, and I quit hanging around with him. His grandma had been paying me to hang out with him anyway."

"Paying you?"

"Yap."

He flicked the cherry of his cigarette butt out with the index finger of the same hand he held it with, and rolled up the butt like a booger and thumped it into the bed of the truck. He would not litter, not even a cigarette butt.

"She gave me a quarter a week."

"A quarter? That's nothing."

"Not then it wasn't. Plus there wasn't anyone else giving me any money. Mom was at work all the time and, other than my time with Vance—people called him by his last name—I was alone. You know what a quarter could get you back then?" I frowned and shrugged. "For a quarter, you could go to a double feature, and get a Coke and a large popcorn. That's what I did with my quarter every week." He drained his beer and tossed the can in the bed of the truck too.

"Hand me a beer," he said. "You can have another one, too, if you want."

I was still nursing the first one. I didn't mind the taste of it, but it wasn't exactly Dr. Pepper.

He drove until the dirt road turned onto a narrow, paved road and the paved road cut straight through a huge, unending repetition of citrus groves. "Those are some big oranges," I said.

"They're navels."

"What are navels?"

Dad pulled the car over.

"Go pull one off that tree there," he said. "Go. Quick. It's stealing."

I hustled out and grabbed the orange. It felt grimy and was harder to pull off than I thought it would be.

"Come on! Pull it to the side." He pulled a phantom orange from the air.

I did as he said and it snapped right off.

I handed the orange to him.

He pointed to the end of it. On one end it came together in what looked just like a person's belly button.

"See. Looks like an outtie, don't it?"

I nodded. "How come you know so much about oranges and stuff?"

"Used to pick fruit with all your aunts and uncles and

some of your cousins, the older ones. We all did it at one time or another. Oranges, grapefruit, lemons… Then we'd go up to Michigan and pick apples. Both your aunts were born in Michigan." He steered the car back on the road and turned it around. "One more stop."

We drove through a neighborhood and another and another and I began to recognize where we were. We were close to my school. Finally he stopped right in front of the school's main entrance.

"Why'd you stop here?"

"Hadn't really gotten a good look at it since coming back."

"A good look at what?"

"The old high school."

"Wait, you went to high school here?"

"Yeah, for one year. The tenth grade. Back then, ninth grade was junior high. We moved back to Hendersonville the summer after my tenth grade and I graduate from high school there."

"You never told me any of that."

"It never came up, I guess." He pointed at the main entrance. "You can't see it from here, but there's a seal, on the ground, once you get through the entrance. The school seal. My first day of school I spit on it."

"Why?"

"I didn't mean to. I hawked up a good one and let it go and it just so happened to land square on the seal. I was standing right in front of it and just hadn't noticed it." He finished a can of beer, tossed it in the back, opened a fresh one. "My luck, the assistant principal — can't remember his name — was standing nearby and saw the whole thing. He detained me. That was his word — 'detain' — and took me into his office where he had an old toothbrush and some kinda cleaner and a washrag. We went back out to the seal and he made me clean and polish the damn thing."

"Man," I didn't know what to say. "They were proud of that thing. You should go spit on it now — no one's looking." I was joking.

Dad looked at me, his face like a bad teenager's.

"Should I?"

I wasn't going to triple-dog dare him, but I didn't see any reason not to.

"Yeah, man. Do it for your tenth-grade self."

He put down his can of beer, glanced around. He got out of the car and ran up to the entrance. He got to the spot and stood there. He looked my way and pointed down at the ground.

"Damn thing's gone!" he yelled. He stood, kind of hangdog, for a moment, shrugged and jogged back to the car.

Seven

THE PARTY WOULDN'T START UNTIL AROUND
ten. I knew nothing about parties, but apparently
real parties didn't start at six or seven—they started
at around ten or eleven. I didn't quite understand
any of this but Cowboy said it had something to do with not
being a "pussy." Josh had a pretty good catalogue of skate
videos on VHS so we hung at his place and watched this
"sick compilation" he had made. He dispassionately
explained to us how he'd done it, but I wasn't really listening.
I couldn't stop thinking about Louise and whether or not
she'd show up at the party, and if she did, what would
happen? What would we do? Also, I kept trying to picture
the party. How many people would be there and what kind
of music would they play? Would there be free alcohol?
Would there be drugs? Was I dressed appropriately? I didn't
want to ask about or mention any of these concerns though,
for fear of being made fun of. I didn't know how any of this

stuff worked, but no one else seemed to be concerned about any of these things.

We watched Josh's video and then we all went skateboarding.

"Karl's apartment is near the high school. We can go skate the school for a while and then head over to his place."

***

We got to the high school at about eight and decided to skate at the pavilion, which stood between the gym and the football stadium. It had wooden picnic tables that were great for grinds, board slides, and for using as a fun box.

After we'd been there for about thirty minutes, we all stopped because we heard a voice we couldn't quite make out.

"You ain't supposed to be out here on yer skateboards, you little shits!"

We all slowly stooped over and grabbed our boards.

"Don't make me call the po-leese!"

The voice came from behind us, from the south, and we all turned and saw a figure, a person walking our way out of the darkness and into the glow of the streetlight.

The voice hooted and laughed. Then the figure, still not too clear, threw something down on the ground and jumped onto it—a skateboard. It was a kid.

"Holy shit!" said Josh. "No way…"

"Is that Spencer…?" said Cowboy.

Ira smiled. He put his board down, jumped on, and started pushing, fast, and when he reached Spencer, he jumped off his board and grabbed him in a bearhug and they both fell to the ground. This is true friendship, I thought. Will anybody ever like me this much?

Ira and Spencer walked back to the rest of us and Ira

grabbed Spencer around the neck, in a headlock, and Spencer grabbed Ira's tit and squeezed. "Keep your damn hands off me!"

"This is the guy we're always saying you look like," said Josh.

Spencer looked at me with a grimace. "I don't see it." He looked down at my board. "Is that the new Ray Barbee?"

"Yeah, how could you tell."

"Spencer is a goddamn savant when it comes to board shapes," said Cowboy.

Spencer looked over at Cowboy. Then he looked at Josh and Ira again.

"I can't believe I'm looking at all you assholes right now."

"So, yeah," said Josh. "You're not in Kansas anymore…"

"Real fucking original," says Spencer. "It's Nebraska. Plus Lincoln is better than this shithole town. You guys are so deprived you don't even know how bad you got it."

"Why are you back?" said Cowboy.

"Well, Cowboy, I missed your mom's hand jobs."

Everyone laughed. I knew it was a joke, but I had no trouble believing that Cowboy's mother had given Spencer a hand job or two.

Turned out Spencer's grandmother had dropped him off downtown and he'd just skated around, hitting all the skate spots, until he found us at the school. He'd told her he'd call her when he knew where he was going to stay the night. We told him about the party and he was in.

"I'll call my old ass grandma when we get there and tell her I'm staying at your house, Josh—if that's okay."

Josh said it was. His parents were very permissive and always let people spend the night. Josh introduced me to Spencer and we shook hands and we gave each other a long look. This is the guy I looked like…

I hung back and followed and listened as the four caught up. We walked down the dark neighborhood roads for several blocks until we got to the entrance to a really big apartment complex, one I'd never actually seen before. It surprised me to see it—three large six-story blocks, heavily lit up, with lots of landscaping too, and a big emerald, shimmering pool in the back of the property. To me, it was a nice place. I couldn't believe a nineteen-year-old guy lived in one of these apartments.

"three-twenty-three," said Ira. I just followed the four in front of me. We walked up to the middle building.

"Building three," said Spencer. "Must be on the second floor."

We found stairs on the back side of the building and slowly walked up. We could hear heavy metal music.

"Metallica. Fucking metalheads," said Josh.

"Their early stuff is good," said Spencer.

Who fucking cares? I thought, but wasn't comfortable enough to speak. I was still the new guy, and here was this new-old guy who seemed to command a lot of respect from the others, almost as if he was older than the rest of them. I was still feeling things out, and now that this Spencer-dude was back I needed to recalibrate. I was in wait-and-see mode.

Ira reached the door first. "Knock, man," said Spencer.

"Do we knock or just go in? Or do we knock and then go in?"

Spencer pushed by and knocked.

"Knock louder," said Cowboy.

But the door opened. A pretty goth girl—died black bob and a Skinny Puppy t-shirt—stood in the doorway smiling.

"Yo," said Josh with a wave.

She giggled and said "Yo" in a deep, mocking tone and stepped aside. "I told you someone was knocking!"

We all walked in, haltingly, unsure, people, on all sides, stood in small clutches—sitting on the floor, leaning against the wall standing in the middle of the living room—and talked and laughed and drank and smoked. Music was loud but not so loud that people had to yell.

The boy-to-girl ratio looked promising. Also, there were girls who looked our age, some of whom I'd never seen before—girls from other high schools, I figured. Everyone there looked our age and older.

"Holy shit," said Josh. "Look! Mudfish."

Sure as shit there she sat on the couch in the living room, square in the middle, two guys on her left and one on her right. They drank from cans of beer. She smiled, awkwardly, and gave a shy wave in our direction. I smiled and quickly turned to see what was happening on the other side of the room. Looking around it became immediately apparent to me that our little group looked out of place, standing in the middle of the room, eyes wide and mouths agape, watching. Somehow we didn't fit in.

A door opened from the back, a bedroom door, and a girl, about eighteen, walked slowly and calmy out. She had a hesitant look in her eye, and she was wearing a Clash shirt and cut-off jeans and in one hand she had a Miller Lite and in the other a black bra. She walked across the living room, like a runway model, to the corner and sat down. She was beautiful, but she didn't look happy. Wounded was the word that came to mind. I imagined frightful things happening in the room she'd come out of. I felt like going over and talking to her but thought better of it. Then the same door opened again and a guy came out wearing nothing but gym shorts. He was tall and blond and somewhat muscular but very ugly in the face. He was eighteen or nineteen but in the face looked much older.

Someone yelled "Karl!" He smiled and nodded, but walked right up to me. Just stood there and stared at me, then at Josh, Cowboy and Spencer. Spencer sort of leant back, looking up at him and looked completely unphased.

"Who the fuck are these grommets?" He pointed at me. "This one looks twelve."

"Grommets?" said Spencer. "Nice fucking mullet and gym shorts, Skid Row."

No one laughed. It was hilarious—really hilarious—but nobody laughed.

"Hand me five beers," said Karl and a short boy, about sixteen, walked quickly into the kitchen.

Two kids our age, dressed liked skinheads, appeared from the kitchen with the first guy, and they were holding beers.

"Give them each a beer," said Karl. They complied. We stood there holding our beers. Karl smiled and held his hands out, dropped them and said, "Now get the fuck out of my apartment," without a hint of malice or anger or mockery in his voice. Everyone but us laughed. We turned and walked out.

As we were walking down the stairs, holding our abject cans of beer, we turned and were met by two girls— Louise and her older sister.

Louise spotted me and her eyes lit up with recognition and she said, "Neil!" We all stopped on the landing and the guys looked at me, somewhat, I suspect, surprised.

I said hey and she asked why we were leaving so early and Spencer piped up.

"Fucking lame party. It's creepy as hell in there." He held up his beer. "We all grabbed a brew and got out of there."

Louise's sister gave us, collectively, an eyeroll. "Look, Lou, I'm heading up. You can stay with these little skater people if you want. Just meet me at the car at eleven."

"Skater people?" said Spencer. "Listen, girl, those…fucking Neanderthal metalheads and dirt rockers up in that apartment are throwing a straight-up creep fest in there. Maybe you should consider hanging with us too… We're pretty fucking top-shelf." I was beginning to see why this guy's return was met with such regard. Spencer winked at her. She let out a labored sigh and walked slowly up the stairs. "Later skate rats!"

"So where we going?" said Louise.

Spencer glanced around, held up his beer. "We all have one beer. We will drink them and we will burp."

"Pavillion?" said Josh.

No one objected. Louise and I hung back a little. Ira glanced back a couple times.

"So did you guys get kicked out?" Louise pulled a red and white pack of cigarettes out of the breast pocket of her denim jacket.

"Yeah. Hey, I didn't know you smoked."

She held the opened pack in my direction.

"Nah. Don't really smoke."

She did not persist. She put the cigarette between her lips, stopped walking, stood perfectly erect, cupped her left hand over her cigarette, and lit it with her right hand. She did not move her body again until she had taken a first drag and glanced at the end of her cigarette. She made smoking look interesting, like a kind of activity, some small thing to do when something to do is needed. She brought a kind of artistic flair to it. You got the feeling she went through the exact same ritual every time, like those Japanese women who have made an art out of pouring a cup of tea. Everything was intentional and premeditated. As a matter of fact, I thought, as we walked and talked and didn't talk, she was like that with everything. She had a real way about her, more than anyone I'd known at that point. It wasn't affectation exactly, but a cultivation of her natural ways. I guess you'd say she had style.

When we got to the pavilion, Spencer and Josh pushed the two picnic tables closer and we all sat on them and drank our beers. Dude and Louise smoked, and they both smoked the same brand of cigarettes. Ira made a point of sitting on the other side of Louise from me. It was becoming clear to me that Ira liked Louise, too, which explained his behavior from the very beginning. But, hey, I thought, he never did anything about it. Here I was making an effort. Let her decide. I wouldn't push it, overdo it, I'd be me and whatever happened would happen. If I got lucky Ira wouldn't be so smart: he'd overdo it and make a fool of himself, or at least, not look so good next to my cool calmness. I was proud of myself for being so uncharacteristically smart.

"I'm kind of glad we got kicked out of that party," I said.

Louise smiled. "I don't really care for parties," she said.

Ira heard and got visibly flustered.

"Me neither," he said. "Parties are lame."

"I don't mind a party," said Louise, "if it kind of organically happens." She straightened her poster and put the palm of a hand-out. "Like this. I'd call this a party. But it just sort of happened. That's the kind of party I like."

At that Spencer burped and held his beer up like a trophy. "I have finished my beer. Let it be known… I have burped."

Josh punched him in the arm and the beer can hit the

ground.

Josh threw his full, unopened beer can at the wall of the handball court and it hissed and exploded. "God! this is fucking bullshit!" He seemed inordinately angry. No one, except for Louise and me, seemed to think it was unusual. I chalked it up to us not really knowing them that well. They'd all been friends since elementary school.

Josh and Spencer decided to go back to Josh's house and watch skate videos. Cowboy just went home alone. Soon it was just Ira, Louise, and me. Louise said she'd better get back to her sister's car, so we walked her back.

The party still raged on. You could hear music, now some kind of industrial, pulsing out of it. We sat on the trunk of her sister's car, which was a late-sixties model Impala, a badass car, and talked a little bit.

"I don't think your sister's coming out," said Ira. "Not for a while, anyway."

Just then the apartment door opened and Mudfish appeared. She was visibly drunk, unsteady on her feet.

"Is that Teresa?" said Louise.

"You mean Mudfish," said Ira.

Louise looked over at Ira. "Mudfish? What's that supposed to mean?" She was glaring now.

Ira looked rattled. "I don't know. It's just what some people call her."

"Well, it sounds mean." Louise hopped off the trunk of the car. I followed.

She cupped her hands around the sides of her face. "Teresa! Is that you?"

Teresa looked down at us.

"Louise!" she said enthusiastically and waved wildly. She leaned over the railing and squinted, "And Ira and the, the new guy…"

"Neil," I said with a quick wave.

"And Neil," she said, making an invisible checkmark in the air with her hand.

"Are you okay, Teresa,?"

"Yes, thank you, Louise. You're so nice Louise." She blew Louise a kiss and went back inside.

Louise turned to Ira and me. She pointed behind her. "Well, dudes. I'm gonna head inside, find my sister, and keep an eye on Teresa. It's been fun." She walked toward the stairs, then stopped and turned around. "See you in school." We watched her walk up and go inside and, after a few quiet moments, we said bye to each other and went our separate ways.

{Part Three}

One

MOSTLY RURAL AND AGRICULTURAL, FRUIT Hollow lay forty-five miles, equidistance, between Tampa (to the southwest) and Orlando (to the northeast). Two fairly large cities with music scenes, skate parks and music stores. By the tenth grade some of my friends had gotten cars, so these cities became more accessible, and our world became a bigger place, a more interesting place, and some of us took full advantage.

Ira, being the most financially flush of us, showed up one Monday, not long after his sixteenth birthday, driving a Mercedes-Benz; a 1966 250se, painted British racing green. For most of us, it was one of the coolest things we'd ever seen.

I went to my first concert in that car. The Circle Jerks with The Weirdos, at the Bourbon Club in Orlando. The Circle Jerks celebrated their tenth anniversary with this tour. 1980-1990. An older kid, a twelfth-grade goth-skater dude named Scott, whose car was in the shop had really wanted to go. He told Ira that he'd pay his way if he gave him a ride. Somehow I managed to scrape together the fifteen-dollar cover and Ira, Scott, Spencer and I all piled into the Green Hornet (our name for Ira's car) and took off for O-town.

Orlando, the real Orlando, was so much different from the Orlando I'd experience on family trips to Disney and Sea World. Downtown Orlando was gritty and tough and by the time we got to The Bourbon that night, kids had mobbed the place. This was, after all, The Circle Jerks.

We parked in a lot a few blocks away and as we got closer we encountered more and more kids our age, mostly punks, but new wave and goth chicks too, and skinheads. In fact, as we got to the façade of the theater, a whole batallion of skinheads stood out front. I'd never seen a skinhead in real life. I'd seen them in magazines and in pictures on album covers and in punk-rock documentaries, but this was different. There were about fifteen of them, all dressed to the 'nines'. Most of them wore bombers and flight jackets and tight jeans and Doc Marten's or combat boots with red or white laces in them. I knew red usually meant American pride and white meant 'white power' or 'white pride', but one skin had green laces in his boots. I nudged Spencer as we walked up to get in line, "Green laces?"

"Eco-skin," he said.

"Eco?"

"Yeah, he's a skinhead who is into ecology." He shrugged and said, "He's probably a vegan too. He'll, like, kick your ass if you litter."

I didn't know what vegan meant, not yet, and suspected Spencer was just messing with me, but I let it go, I didn't want to look like a total ignorant ass.

"Interesting," I said.

On the other side of the entrance were some

seriously dressed-up punks—huge dayglo mohawks and leatherjackets or denim jackets—or both—with patches all over them. They wore t-shirts of bands I'd never even heard of. Standing, talking to a punk wearing a sleeve-less denim jacket, and whose arms were covered in tattoos, was a short older guy, about thirty-five, I guessed. He had dark circles around his eyes, dreadlocks to his waist, and wore big baggy cut off army shorts and a pair of beat-up Chuck Taylors.

"Dude!" Spencer said. "Look."

"I see him," I said. "He's an old guy. That's so cool."

"That's not just any old guy. That's Keith Morris."

"No shit!" I realized he was right. It was him, the singer for The Circle Jerks, just hanging out before the show, talking to some punks.

"See, dude," said Spencer. "That's why punk rock is so fucking awesome."

I knew exactly what he meant. No explanation needed. Jon Bon Jovi didn't stand outside and talk to his fans. David Lee Roth didn't do that. But Keith Fucking Morris did. Punk rock was not about being a star or being worshiped by people. It was against all that shit. And here was living proof.

"Let's go say hi to him," said Spencer.

I just looked at him.

"What? Dude, he's just a punk. He's not Jesus." He elbowed me. "Come on." He walked toward him, and I followed slowly.

When Spencer got next to him, Keith Morris and the punk kid quit talking, and looked at Spencer. Spencer put out his hand, and Keith took it. He didn't exactly have a smile on his face, but he didn't look pissed off either. I stood and watched.

"It's a, uh, lifelong dream to see you guys," said Spencer.

"Lifelong, huh?" said Keith. I could tell by looking at his face that a delicate balancing act was going on in his mind, one that kept him from going into total sarcastic asshole mode. He wanted to be nice to this scared kid, but his natural inclination was to say something biting. "Well, that's cool, man. Thanks for coming to see us old bastards." He kind of punched Spencer on the shoulder. Spencer smiled and nodded.

Keith Morris looked around Spencer, getting a better look at me. "You okay over there, little straight-edge guy?" Now he smiled.

"Yeah, I'm not really straight-edge, though," I said. "You were in Black Flag."

Now he let loose a laugh that sounded like moist sandpaper being dragged across chrome.

"Sorry," I said.

Spencer smacked me across the head and said, "Yeah, my buddy here is kind of a retard."

The show was intense. I had nothing to compare it to, because it was my first, but I was blown away. We slammed and stage dived and sang along, and there were cute girls there and scary skinheads and old punks and all of us were sweating and singing and dancing and no one fought or got mad and it was amazing. A total youth-culture mind-blow.

We were hooked. Other shows soon followed. We'd go see anyone. We went to shows in Orlando or Tampa—even Melbourne and St. Pete a few times—every chance we got: Gwar, Death, Slayer, Fugazi, All, Rancid, The Cramps, Shelter, Faith No More, Pink Lincolns, The Queers, Screeching Weasel, Green Day, Bad Religion, Helmet, Skinny Puppy, Godflesh, Primus… We went to every show we could.

We went to all the skate parks Tampa and Orlando

had too. Almost every weekend, it seemed, a skate park, or a show. At the weekends we stayed in town and we'd all meet up somewhere, somehow, and skate and ride bikes (by now Burt and Sam, these local freestyle bikers, were hanging with us too) and listen to music and raise hell.

And tenth grade seemed to have passed this way. A year of weekends. I could barely remember the school-filled week-days. It felt like the beginning of an amazing time of my life, even as it was happening. Things changed so much in such a short time. By the end of the school year I had a tight group of friends, and we were beginning to know what we wanted and how to get it, or so we thought. I almost never thought about Sam, Sean or CJ: or Nat, or Hill; but when I did I felt sad. I called CJ a few times during the first six months or so of living in Summardale, but each phone call got shorter and shorter and by the last phone call we both seemed to have run out of things to say.

That Christmas, I asked for a bass guitar and an amp, and to my amazement, I got both. Somehow dad and mom had scraped up enough to get them. They were nothing special. They were used and probably from a pawn shop, but I didn't care. They worked and I was so excited: it didn't matter. Too bad I had almost no idea how to play music.

Many of us got instruments that Christmas, and the ones who didn't, well, they could be singers. Don't wanna sing? You could be a roadie? You can draw? Okay, you'll make fliers. Whatever. Everyone could do something. No one was excluded.

Two

BY THE START OF THE SUMMER, I COULD play the bass well enough to follow along with a guitar player. All I did was play the root note of a power chord, but it was enough for now. Ira had already been playing guitar for two years, and we played together as often as possible. He taught me how to play bass and tried teaching me how to tune the thing, but it was no use. I had no ear at all. He always had to tune it for me. "Now that school's over, we have all summer. We can play every day. Just keep practicing and practicing."

Spencer played guitar, too, and though Ira had more technical facility, Spencer was more creative and came up with the best riffs. Josh, who had been in marching band for a year now, could play drums, even though he didn't have a drum set. Spencer, Ira, Josh and I played together as often as we could, and Josh saved every cent he got to put toward a drum kit, but in the meantime he banged on pots and boxes and whatever else he thought made a cool sound.

"You need to get a fucking job, dude," Spencer told Josh. "Otherwise it's gonna take you forever to save up for a drum kit."

An older guy Josh knew had a kit he told him he'd sell for three hundred dollars if he could get the money. It wasn't anything special, a three-piece Tama, with a ride, a hi-hat, and one crash symbol. But it was in pretty good shape, and three hundred was actually a steal.

"I don't want a job. I'll figure something out."

"Well, I'm getting sick of making up songs so that you can play along to them on a five-gallon bucket. And you," he turned his attention to me. "Your amp sucks, man. Your bass is passible. But that amp just isn't loud enough. I'm serious here, people. If we want to be in a real band—like play shows and shit—then we need to quit fucking around."

Spencer *was* serious, too. He was more serious than any of us would ever be. Also, I think he was feeling left behind. A pretty good punk band in the area had already formed and started playing small shows. They were called Transmission Cancelled—not a great name, but they were tight. They were kids, a little older than us, mostly eleventh graders and one twelfth grader, who were from a rich part of Summerdale, Cypress Estates, while we were mostly broke-ass Fruit Hollow kids. They played super-fast thrash punk. All their songs were around a minute long. They had already put out a seven-inch record on their own label: Vermithrax Records. Their songs were so short that the record had twelve songs on it. The first time you saw them you were completely confused. Their record, which had pictures of dead bodies, soldiers and anarchy symbols all over it, was so punk sounding. Total aggressive punk. You expected them to have mohawks and wear leather and boots. But they dressed like preps: khakis, duck head shirts, and vans. The vans were the most punk thing about their look. It was like a uniform. They all dressed the same—like a bunch of rich kids, which is what they were. It was completely disorientating, but the juxtaposition worked.

We went to see them one night. You could tell Spencer was jealous and pissed off. They were awesome, looked cool and sounded great. They were one step ahead. Spencer knew he couldn't be in that band, but he wanted to be in a band like it.

"I'm giving you guys a month to get your shit together or I'm looking elsewhere for bandmates," said Spencer. "I'm not fucking around. You guys are acting like Cowtown shitheads—and you are—but you don't have to be. We need to be taking this as serious as our school-work. We need to be serious if we want to be in a band that plays shows and puts out records and gets chicks. Dude, girls will like you if you are in a band, even a shitty band. Look at Transmission Cancelled. They have a stupid name and dress like assholes and sometimes there are more girls at their shows than there are dudes." Spencer looked kind of angry. "You all have one month."

I damn sure wasn't getting a job, not one where you had to fill out an application and wear some bullshit uniform. To me Spencer's ambition didn't fit in with his supposed punk-rock ethos. I didn't want to work at a restaurant, washing dishes, or a grocery store, bagging groceries. Working for some rich asshole was not punk.

It turned out my new uncle, Paul, ran his own landscape and lawn maintenance company and he sometimes put twerps like me to work when one of his guys called in sick or when he got a really big job and needed an extra hand. Paul and Aunt Belinda lived about a mile and a half away from us so we saw them frequently.

One day after school I asked my dad if I could ask Paul to consider having me work for him. School was over, and the summer was a busy time for landscapers. Dad said he didn't mind me asking, as long as I was serious.

"He's not gonna tolerate any fucking around. If he takes you on, he's gonna expect you to work just as hard as anyone else."

I told Dad I understood and I'd work my ass off.

"It's easy for a short-timer to outwork a full-timer," he said. "Full-timers are there forty or more hours a week, so they tend to pace themselves. A little piss-ant like you, who comes in and works every once in a while, you better work harder than the others. Otherwise you're just worthless."

One Friday after dinner I skated over to Paul and Belinda's place. They rented a doublewide trailer in a decent looking trailer park in sight of Lake Carr. The front door was open and the screen door was shut against the bugs. I knocked on the aluminum frame of the screen door and it rattled.

"Git hell out of here!" said Paul.

"You ain't even know who's at the door," said Belinda.

She walked up to the screen and squinted down at me.

"That you Neil?" Belinda had terrible eyesight but refused to wear glasses.

"Yes, ma'am."

She opened the screen and I stepped up into the trailer. Paul was sprawled out on the couch, wearing nothing but blue jeans, unbuttoned at the top, and his requisite cap on backwards.

"What's up, buddy?" He didn't budge.

"Nothing."

Belinda went back to washing dishes in the small kitchen, visible from the living room.

"You hungry?" she said.

"No, thank you."

A WWF wrestling match was on TV. The Iron Sheik had Sgt. Slaughter in his dreaded Camel Clutch. I didn't care for wrestling, but knew all the wrestlers' names from it always being on at everyone's house.

Paul, this man who was technically my uncle, but not a blood relative, had been incarcerated many times, as a child and as an adult. For the first time, I noticed a tattoo on his trunk: a tiny red heart with a dagger through it.

"How's your momma and daddy, doing?" said Paul.

"Fine," I said. "I was wondering something."

By now Belinda was finished with the dishes and she sat in a recliner with can of Busch in hand, watching the wrestling. She seemed into it. She made short guttural sounds to go along with their moves, and occasionally uttered her approval or disapproval, "Nope. Wouldn't do that.... Christ!... Yep... Told ya!... Whoops..." Stuff like that.

"I'm trying to scratch together some money and wondered if you needed any help at work. I'll do anything you need done, and I'm a hard worker."

He leaned forward on the couch and took off his cap and scratched his head and then slapped it back on.

"Matter of fact, I could use some help." He looked over at Belinda, who was paying attention to us now, and he winked at her. Belinda was wearing some kind of a nightgown, and you could tell that she probably didn't have anything on underneath it. She was a big lady, my dad's youngest sister, but she was probably close to fifty. Paul was lean and handsome in a Cool Hand Luke kind of way. You couldn't help but wonder what the two of them were doing together. She was plenty old enough to be his mother. I'd recently heard my own mother voice her misgivings to my dad. "It doesn't seem healthy, does it?" she said.

It was a Sunday, and we were in the car, headed to the Sahwoklee County Flea Market where we were meeting Paul and Belinda. "I mean, they do seem to genuinely love each other—or, at least, have affection for one another—but it really is more of a mother-son relationship." My dad, on the other hand, didn't seem bothered. "They're two grown people. They can do whatever they want, as long as they aren't hurting anybody."

"That's great," I said to Paul. "When would you want me to start?"

"Could you work a few hours this Saturday?"

"Yes, of course."

"Could you be here at six in the morning, sharp? That's when we leave. I like to get started early. Don't take long for it to be hotter than a double-peckered goat out there."

I looked over at Belinda and she rolled her eyes. I'd forgot about how early he liked to get to work. That was my least favorite part. But, I'd still have Sunday to sleep in.

"Yep," I said.

"All right. I'll see you then." He leaned back, and we all fell silent for a while, watched the wrestling, a batch of commercials, and when wrestling came back on I excused myself.

As I skated home I realized that Paul and I had not discussed wages. This somewhat worried me, with his being a convict and all. Could I even trust him to pay? But we were family. I figured he'd be fair. If not, my dad would kick his ass.

***

Monday, at school, when I told Spencer I'd secured a job with my uncle, he punched me in the shoulder and hissed at me. "That's it, you son of a bitch! Working man! We're on our way. We should go up to Jimison's Music Store after school and look at amps. I've already got a bass amp picked out for you. It's a hundred watt Ampeg, used, but in great shape. I've already tried it out. Has a beautiful sound."

***

Spencer, Josh and I skated to Jimison's, in downtown Fruit Hollow. We looked at instruments and equipment. Everything was so expensive, even the used stuff. The amp Spencer wanted me to buy was three hundred and fifty bucks. He was right, it sounded beautiful. They gave me a Fender Jazzman to plug into it and goof around on it. The combination of the super high-quality bass and the expensive amp created a lovely, crisp sound. I'd never heard anything like it.

"Even your shitty bass will sound great plugged into this bad boy," said Spencer. "Imagine if you had this bass too." He put his hand on the headstock. The price tag, dangling off the end of it, read $800. It might as well have been $25,000.

From a far-off corner to the right came some crashing and thumping. We turned and looked and saw Josh, his hands holding onto two symbols with a sheepish grin on his face.

We skated back to Josh's room and listened to music. Finally Spencer had to leave. "All these bands, if you really think about it, suck. Except, The Minutemen. You should listen to them as often as possible, Neil. Mike Watt's bass-playing is the best." He picked up his board and walked out of Josh's room.

***

The music thing was great, but my life was going in too many directions for me to be as single-mindedly into the band as Spencer was. Though Louise and I didn't use the terms, girlfriend or boyfriend, and we didn't say we were 'going out or dating,' we were spending lots of time together. Neither of us had a car, but there were others who did and we managed to find ourselves in said cars, usually in a backseat making out and pawing at each other intensely. Ira, you could tell, hated it, but he went along with things. It had started the last week of school. We'd often take off after last bell—a batch of us—and hit a skate spot, skate for a while, then go to McDonald's or Taco Bell or Denny's and sit and waste time, talk about summer plans—shows we hoped to go to, skate spots in nearby towns we hadn't hit yet. But now summer break was here and Louise and I wanted to spend as much time together as possible. She'd be gone soon—to her aunt and uncle's in Vermont, until a week before school started back up again. Vermont might as well have been on the moon.

The last week of school that year I was in Mass Media, which was taught by Mr. Mulroney. Mulroney was a cool guy. We mostly watched classic movies and talked about them. In that class I sat next to a guy named Wayne, a metalhead guy with shoulder length blond hair who wore a black leather jacket almost every day. Over the course of the semester we'd really hit it off. I went to his house a few times and hung out in his room with him, listened to music and talked about random shit. He was a smart guy and had a different perspective than most of my other friends. He had a thoughtful way of seeing things. He was the first person I ever met who was a vegan.

We had some downtime in Mulroney's class one day and noticed a stack of old high school yearbooks in a far corner of the room. We started flipping through them when I thought of something.

"Hey, my dad went to school here."

"Mine too."

We did the math and figured out which yearbooks would have our dads in them. There was one nineteen-sixty-eight and we found both our dads in that one. His dad was a senior that year, so we found him in the front of the book, in the bigger pictures. His dad had a huge grin on his somewhat chubby face and his light hair was done in a pompadour. We chuckled and stared for a while.

"This is so weird," said Wayne. "I've never seen this before." He shook his head like he had to break a spell. "Let's find your dad."

My dad was a junior. There he was. Jet black hair, parted to the side, and big, black-framed glasses. He looked big and angry. No smile at all, like he hated everything about that moment. He looked like a chubby Clark Kent.

"My dad played football," said Wayne, and he found the football team's group picture. They stood in two rows, behind a sign that said Fruit Hollow Hornets. They were in suits. His dad had been a defensive lineman. Same smile on his face, and standing next to him, was the guy who played center, my dad.

"Dude! Is that you're dad?"

"Yeah. It is. He never told me he played football in high school."

I couldn't believe it for some reason. My dad had never expressed an interest in any sports and had never mentioned playing football in high school. We'd never watched a football game together or thrown a football in the yard or anything. To my knowledge, I'd never even heard him say the word 'football.'

"My dad doesn't give a shit about football either," said Wayne. "My dad doesn't seem to be interested in anything, to tell you the truth. He goes to work and he comes home, eats dinner, watches the news and goes to bed." He closed the yearbook and sat it on top of the stack. "We barely even talk to be honest."

"My dad doesn't really have any interests either. Music, a little, I guess. He likes old movies. He listens to records a lot, and watches a lot of TV. That's it, though."

"Shit!" said Wayne. "I don't even know what my dad and I would talk about if we did."

***

After school that day I walked Louise home. She only lived six blocks from school and her parents were pretty cool about letting me hang out there for a couple hours. We sat in her room. She smoked cigarettes while we listened to music and talked.

She had a huge walk-in closet which she'd turned into a darkroom and developed her own photographs. We'd sometimes sit in there with the darkroom light on and talk, our faces aglow with a low red light.

"Do your parents have any interests?" I asked her. "Like, do they do anything interesting, besides the usual stuff, like working and cooking and mowing the lawn?"

"They both read a lot. And my dad is obsessed with Ole Miss football. All football season he walks around the house in this disintegrating Ole Miss jersey. It's disgusting."

"See neither of my parents are obsessed with anything, as far as I can tell. They just do the usual stuff. I don't understand that. It's like they have no life."

Louise turned the florescent light on and we sat there

blinking.

"I think most people, once they get older and have kids, just lose interest in things. They sort of give up on their aspirations. It's normal, I think. That's why I'm not having kids. I think I'm going to go to college and then graduate school—get a degree in literature or something—and then move somewhere remote—Minnesota or Maine—and teach at a small college and have my own little apartment. Just read and teach and travel and take pictures in the summer."

I'd never thought about my life that way. I'd never considered what I'd actually want to do—only what I'd probably *end up* doing. What did I want to do? Everything I thought of seemed impossible or ridiculous. I couldn't be a pirate or adventurer. Those weren't real things, and I wasn't going to be in a band because I could already tell I had no musical talent. The only thing that made any sense, it seemed, for a guy like me was the military. My dad had been in the Air Force—in fact I'd been born on an Air Force base—but I couldn't imagine myself doing that either. I couldn't imagine myself doing anything. Maybe that was my problem—no imagination. Maybe I came from a no-imagination family.

***

That evening, at the dinner table, I asked my dad why he never told me he played football in high school. He froze for a second, after putting a bite of meatloaf in his mouth, like he'd been caught in a lie.

"I don't know," he said with his mouth full of meatloaf. "I guess I never thought you'd be interested."

"You talk about a lot of things I'm not interested in."

"True." He took a sip of beer. "I guess *I* never was interested. I didn't really like it. The only reason I played was because I was big and the PE coach, who was also the football coach, said they needed a center. He asked me if I wanted on the team. I said sure. I didn't even have to try out. And I got to wear one of those letterman jackets. Girls liked it…"

"Girls…?" mom said, and James chuckled.

"I guess I just wondered because you don't even watch football."

Then he got a far-off look and tilted his head to the right.

"How did you know I played football in high school?"

I told him about the stack of yearbooks.

"I never did get any yearbooks. We were always too poor. Couldn't afford it."

"I could probably bring you one home if you want."

"Nah, I don't need one."

Mom said yes, and James nodded.

"I'd love to see one," mom added.

"I'll see if I can get one," I said.

Later that night James came into my room. I was listening to music and working on my skateboard, tightening my trucks, just tinkering, really. He sat down next to me and said nothing. The music stopped—it was The Misfits.

"I hate your music," he said.

I smiled and flipped the tape over.

"Could you bring one of those yearbooks home," he said. "I'd like to see those old pictures of dad."

I told him I'd try. He said, "Cool," and left my room, swinging his arms, and with a particular pep to his step. I never did bring home a yearbook.

Three

I WORKED HARD THAT SUMMER. IT WAS PHYSICAL labor in extreme heat. I'd done physical work before, for a day or two, here and there, with Corley and with my dad, but I'd never had what amounted to a full-time job, which is what this job was with Uncle Paul. He didn't go easy on me, and following his example, neither did the other two men on his crew, Gabe and Rene, who were Mexicans in their early thirties. We would become good buddies, but for the first week they were distant and tough on me. You couldn't blame them. They were hardworking men, with families, and in I walked, a high school kid and nephew to their boss. They wanted to make sure I wasn't there to coast. They wanted to make sure I was worth a damn. They wanted to see how hard a worker I was. It's only natural. I didn't blame them.

***

The band was coming along too. We'd settled on the name 'Philisteens' because Spencer thought it sounded cool. A friend of his mother's, back in Nebraska, used to say it all the time. Any time someone didn't know some factoid or bit of trivia, he'd refer to them as a 'Philistine.' According to Spencer it meant *uncultured swine* and was also a biblical tribe who quarreled with the Israelites. I didn't care for the name, and I could tell no one else did either, but we didn't have anything better. The best I'd come up with was Knucklehead, and all anyone else could come up with was common household items: doorjamb, broomstick, backsplash, and the like. Ira said, "How about Philis-TEENS. Philisteens. Like, you know. We're teenagers. Makes it more punk." Spenser's face lit up and he punched Ira.

By the end of the school year we had three mostly decent songs, all three under the three-minute mark. It was Spencer's rule. "Nothing worth a damn is any longer than three minutes," he was fond of saying. "This is a punk band, not The goddamn Grateful Dead." No one voiced disapproval of this notion, although I know I wouldn't have stood by his statement. I got it. I understood what it meant for our band. We were creating an aesthetic and a style, but, at the time, one of my favorite pieces of music was "Time" by Pink Floyd, from Dark Side of the Moon, a song that comes in at around seven minutes, and, to my mind, was pretty godamn close to perfection. Not that I would have admitted any of that to Spencer. His measure of all things good, musically, was The Minutemen's master piece, Double Nickels on the Dime, an album whose average song time was around a minute and a half. So we all knew where he was coming from, and since he had assumed the mantle of fearless bandleader, we let all his pronouncement stand when it came to how the band should sound. The rest of us were just happy to be there. We just wanted to stand in front of people and play, and hopefully have girls like us because of it. We didn't give a shit how long the songs were.

***

My first day of work with Uncle Paul's crew was tough. I was nothing to Rene and Gabe but a scrawny little shit that didn't deserve what they viewed as a pretty cush job. Rene was the older of the two—in is late thirties—and, despite his mouth being completely devoid of teeth, was almost always smiling. The skin on the sides of his face reminded me of those aerial pictures of the Mississippi delta you see in geography books; lines upon lines going off in various directions—smile lines. He looked so much older than he was.

I did every shit job that first day. I toted all the heavy stuff and I manned the wheelbarrow. I mowed the areas that could not be reached with the riding mower. I pulled weeds, cleaned out beds and dug drainage ditches. Rene and Gabe had it pretty easy. They spent most of the day riding mowers or casually walking around with leaf-blowers on their backs. I figured it was like hazing. I needed to pay my dues. I didn't complain and I acted like it was all above board. Paul didn't say anything either. He knew what was happening, but I think he got a kick out of watching it all go down. I think he was proud of how well I took it all.

That was my approach the whole first week. I kept on like I was their servant. By the end of day two, I didn't even wait to be told. A shit job would come up and I'd jump in and get to it. The rougher and dirtier and harder the better. I relished it. I had become a masochist. Pile it on, fuckers! I got this shit! Gators? Water-moccasins? Shit… I ain't scared.

But I was scared. And, in reality, I was at my breaking

point.

There are many lakes in Lawrence county, but Lake Picaro, its largest, lies like a sleeping giant in profile in the center of town. I've seen ariel photographs of it. It's a beast. Back then it was rumored to be, at its deepest, in excess of three-hundred feet deep. Cars and semitrucks supposedly had at some point in time been sunk into it. One of my uncle's clients, the one he was most proud of, had a lakefront home on Lake Picaro.

We pulled onto a long, serpentine driveway and my uncle let the truck roll slowly, respectfully up the drive to the end where the house was. The house was not tall, but it was long, sleek and sexy.

"Take a look at that beauty," said Paul.

"It's a nice house."

"Keep looking," he said. "It's more than nice." He picked up his clipboard. "I'll tell you something about it."

I kept looking and I realized that the roof was kind of shaped like a lean-to or bleachers or a ski-launch.

"It's got two famous things about it."

"Yeah," I said, and waited.

He put his clipboard down and grabbed his pack of Reds off the dash and lit one.

"Guess who the owner is?"

"I have no idea. The mayor or governor or someone like that?"

"You got no imagination, boy." He blew a stream of blue smoke.

"I'll give you a hint." He put his cigarette between his lips, slicked his blond bangs to the side. "Cannonball Run."

Burt Reynolds came immediately to mind, so that's who I said.

He stubbed out his cigarette in the ashtray. "That's

right," he said.

"Wow! He lives there?"

"No, I said he owns it. No one lives there. I mean, he rents it out to people sometimes, but it's vacant most of the time. He comes down a couple weeks a year and stays in it." He paused and sighed. "He's a Florida boy, you know."

I wanted to tell everyone about this. I thought about band practice.

"The second thing I'll just tell you, because you won't know shit about it anyway. This beautiful, minimalist home was designed by Frank Lloyd, Goddamn, Wright. But you don't know who that is, do you?"

"Name's familiar."

"He's America's most famous architect. Did these prairie style homes." He saw the blankness on my face and shook his head and then punched me in the arm, hard. "Fucking barbarian."

***

I put on the hip-waiters, got the trimmer and walked down to the lake shore the backyard dissolved into. The grass was high, hadn't been cut in months, I guessed. The engine cranked on the first pull and I walked down into the water, about knee high and started to cut down the grass as close to water level as possible.

I found a rhythm and zoned out: back and forth, back and forth, with the trimmer—left and right, left and right, and I cut the thick watergrass down as far out as I could, until I was standing a little over waist high. I stood and surveyed my work and saw a small circular ripple about forty feet out in front of me. I squinted. Out of the center of the ripple came a wavy line moving in my direction. I quickly realized it was a snake. I turned halfway and threw the trimmer up onto the lake-shore. He moved steadily in my direction, weaving back and forth, almost slowly, but fast enough that I felt hurried. I backed up, unable to take my eyes off the creature. The hip-waiters were heavy. I lost my balance and fell back. I screamed and began to crawl up the shore as quickly as I could. Once out, I ran as fast as I could, until I was on the back porch of the house. I stood there dripping and in shock.

Rene appeared around the corner. He was eating a banana. He stopped when he saw me.

"Que es esto?" He chewed slowly and walked forward.

"A goddamned water-moccasin."

He looked towards the lake. He pointed, banana in hand. "That?"

There it was, popping up out of the water, like a cormorant, and weaving its way back towards the middle.

"Yes! That's it. Jesus, it was coming right at me, coming for me. It was an attack."

He smiled, took the last bite of the banana, and threw the peel into some brush, and the snake, startled, darted under water.

"That's a water snake, bro. Harmless."

"It's a snake in the water, man. My brain went straight to moccasin."

"Your brain don't know shit, cuz."

He went on to explain to me the difference. He explained that moccasins are bigger and fatter than water snakes, and had a very distinct way of swimming, arrow-shaped heads way out of the water.

"Still," he said. "Water snakes will bite you, so better safe than sorry, I guess." He winked at me. He was trying to make me feel better.

At the end of the work-day, Friday, they dropped me

off at the house. Paul paid me out of pocket, and his payment turned out to be fair—fifty bucks a day, $250 a week. I went in, showered, and went straight to bed and slept straight through the night, dreams free of nightmarish snake encounters, and didn't wake until a little after nine on Saturday morning.

***

I worked until the penultimate week of summer. Each Friday I'd put money down on a Fender Jazzman and a 100-watt-Ampeg amplifier. I had them paid off by the second to last pay-day. I had no money to show for shit otherwise, but it didn't matter because I had legitimate equipment now, and my playing seemed to immediately improve. The Fender Jazzman was the most beautiful thing I'd ever put my hands on. Its action was like greased owl shit.

By this time we had eight songs and we decided to invite people to our practice sessions.

Spencer invited Transmission Cancelled over and two of them showed up—Reese and Frigg—probably more out of guarded curiosity than anything else. They wanted to see if we were any competition for them. Reese was the guitar player and singer and Frigg was the bass player.

Reese and Frigg sat on the ratty couch along the garage door and watched with folded arms. Occasionally their heads would bob, in unison, and a smile appeared here and there, but they were pretty reserved. After we played our last song, we all sat around and bullshitted.

"So, what do you think?" said Josh. Spencer punched Josh in the shoulder for being so direct.

Reese looked at Frigg and they smiled.

"Not bad," said Reese, who was clearly the mouthpiece of the band.

"Pretty good," said Frigg.

"Not bad? Pretty good?" Said Spencer.

"Reminds me of early Circle Jerks," said Reese, "Red Tape and shit like that."

"Is that a fucking compliment?" said Spencer. The rest of us laughed nervously.

"Well," said Reese, "I guess that depends on how you feel about early Circle Jerks."

"How do *you* feel about early Circle Jerks?" said Spencer.

"It's the closest thing to Black Flag without being Black Flag…"

"And I guess you're the fucking expert on early punk," said Ira. Ira and Reese had been friends for a long time, so he felt comfortable challenging him.

"More of a fucking expert than you, Bad Religion boy."

They both smiled.

"I don't get it. What's wrong with Bad Religion?" said Josh.

"It ain't punk," said Frigg in a slow drawl. He didn't dip or chew, but something about his mouth made you think he did.

"That's right," said Reese.

After more playful insults, Reese said that they were playing a show at a small club in Lakesburg called The Paisley Giraffe the following Saturday and asked if we wanted to open for them. They're opening band had cancelled. Spencer said yes immediately and added, "But don't get used to it— you guys will be opening for us soon."

After Reese and Frigg left we all went nuts jumping and cheering at the prospect of out first real show.

"But, seriously," said Spencer. "We gotta nail this shit or it'll be our first and last show. We gotta be pro, man—

tight as shit. We gotta practice as much as possible before that fucking show." And we did.

We practiced the Friday before the show—played our whole set three times in a row—and we were feeling great. "We're gonna blow the roof off that place," said Josh. "I feel like we might even get laid."

"You probably won't," said Spencer, "but the rest of us might."

The Paisley Giraffe, dumb name notwithstanding, seemed like a great place for a first show, like the type of place where you got your feet wet. We all felt that way. We were ready.

Four

LOUISE AND I WERE PRETTY OFFICIAL NOW. We spent as much time together as possible. As for the band, our first real show was coming up. We were going to open for Transmission Cancelled at The Paisley Giraffe. The Giraffe, as we quickly came to call it, was a record store owned by this guy named Owen Harris, who had been in the Marines and was in his mid-twenties. He chain-smoked, wore thick glasses, and was always tinkering away on amps and instruments in his shop. He really took to all the local high school kids and, when Reese asked, was quick to agree to start having weekend shows. This inaugural show would be Philisteens, Transmission Cancelled, and this sort of goth band from Lakesburg called Trance Macabre. We didn't like the idea of a goth band playing with us and Transmission, but Reese quickly convinced the rest of us.

"Dude, just wait and see. You'll be happy Trance

Macabre is there, trust me."

***

Reese was right. Trance Macabre drew a crowd we'd never seen before, and many of them were girls, Lakesburg Girls, as we came to call them. These Lakesburg girls had a completely different way about them. They weren't like Fruit Hollow or Summerdale girls. Before we went on, Josh and I were out back of the Giraffe with Owen, leaning on the hood of his shitty car, while he smoked a joint.

"How have I never met any of these girls before?" said Josh.

"Lakesburg is twenty miles away and only a few of you shits have cars, man." He pointed the joint at Josh and, to my surprise, he took it and took a drag of it, coughed, and handed it to me. I followed suit. It burned my throat.

"True," said Josh. "They're not like the girls that hang around us—the few that do."

Louise and her friends were boyish, which was part of their appeal. They eschewed all of the typical female stuff. They wore lots of denim and dressed like us. They were more punk-grunge than new wave or goth or whatever. They were cool. These Lakesburg girls were cool too, but they wore dresses, make-up, carried purses and they all smoked clove cigarettes—or pretended to smoke clove cigarettes. The girls who had been hanging around us were badass and these Lakesburg girls were not qualitatively better or worse, but they were different, and different is disruptive.

We finished the joint with Owen and I started feeling high right away. I then began to realize that was maybe a bad thing.

Spencer walked out the back door and took a look at us and I could tell he was pissed. "Dude, I can smell it. We're about to play our first show and you two get high? Bullshit…" He looked at Owen. "You should be ashamed. Getting high school kids stoned."

Owen flicked him off and smiled.

We all went inside. It was dark and smokey. I lingered in the makeshift backstage area and looked around. To the left of the stage, sitting in a row on two couches were the Lakesburg girls, looking cool, wearing mostly black, except for one, a girl who Spencer had told me was named Samantha. She was in stark contrast to the rest, but she seemed like the de-facto leader, seemed to be the one the others looked up to. Unlike the others, she did not have a short black bob hair-cut, but shoulder length natural blond hair. She wore an orange button up top, cut off denim shorts and oxblood Doc Martens. I caught her staring back at me and I grinned back at her. She smirked and turned her head. She whispered something to the tall brunet sitting to her right and then they both giggled and looked back at me. "Oh, shit," I thought. "What did I do?" I felt like an idiot and being high didn't help with that. She was out of my league, anyway, I thought. She looked to me like she should be dating a tall muscular surfer-dude or something. I wasn't even sure what she was doing here among all these punks, goths, skate rats and freaks. She looked too well-adjusted. Still, I couldn't help looking at her, and the whole night I kept track of her, made sure I knew where she was.

We sounded pretty good when we played. People danced and we didn't make any major mistakes—none that anyone could notice, anyway. Transmission Cancelled, though, they killed it. They were so tight and seemed almost intuitive. We pulled it off, made it seem like we knew what we were doing, sure, but they were flat out good. We were still figuring things out, but they were there. They looked so cool too. They did things in unison, had charisma and just looked right up there. After TC played a lot of people gathered out back, smoked and drank from quarts of beer that Owen or one of his other friends had bought. At one point I went to the bathroom and when I came back out Samantha was standing exactly next to where I had been. She had been watching me walk back to my spot. It was almost as if she'd saved it for me. I pictured her shooing people away who tried to stand there, like a theatre usher or something.

I leaned against the wall and turned to her.

"My name's Neil."

She raised her right eyebrow, like a Bond villain, and smirked. "I know who you are." She put her hand out. "Sam." She had a raspy voice, sounded like she'd just woken up.

"I know who you are," I mimicked, eyebrow raised and all.

She tilted her head back and laughed. I felt like she was imitating a twenty-six-year-old actress. But, still. She was actually beautiful. She was, I could say, the first beautiful girl who'd ever wanted to talk to me.

"I've heard you're a pretty cool guy," she said.

"I don't know what that means."

"See, it's true," she said. "I've also heard you're dating that *Louise* girl."

There was something very dismissive in the way she'd said *that Louise girl*, which surprised me. I'd never heard a girl refer to another girl that way.

"Where is she now?"

"She had to go out of town with her parents. First to Vermont, to visit an aunt. Now she's in Homestead. Her dad's a building contractor and he's had to go down there a lot ever since Hurricane Andrew."

"Fascinating." She put her hand back out for me to shake. "Well, let me know when you don't have a girlfriend anymore."

I shook her hand and watched her walk away. What the hell was that? I thought. Was she asking me to break up with my girlfriend?

All of Transmission Cancelled walked up to where I was standing, like a gang. I realized I was now surrounded by them.

"What's up, son?" said Reese. He nodded at the others. "Pretty good turn out."

Spencer sidled up to me to get closer to Reese, who I gathered he saw as his counterpart.

"Yeah, pretty good," said Spencer. He looked around like he was assessing the crowd.

Reese looked back at me. "Saw you talking to Sam." He grinned.

"Yeah. She's pretty cool."

"Son, she's crazy."

"How do you know her?"

"Let's just say I know her well enough to know." He slapped my shoulder and they all walked off together.

"Well, that's illuminating," I said. Reese heard me, turned around and smiled at me in response, and kept walking.

"What a bunch of assholes…" said Josh, and we all laughed except Spencer.

***

With Lousie I had a solid relationship, but there didn't seem to be much in the way of it progressing when Sam started showing up at every Philisteens show. She didn't even really do anything—she didn't have to. It was all looks and innuendo and body language. I was getting my first glimpse of a real professional at work. I'd never seen the likes of it.

Women—young ladies—doing their thing. Most men—young men—truly are much less sophisticated than most young women. In general, we try to stay out of trouble, and to avoid confrontation and will go to great lengths to do so. But, eventually, things come to a head—they always do—and things get ugly and, at times, violent. Men don't like to fuck around and, consequently, there is often an all-or-nothing aspect to the way we operate. It's different with some women. They are slick, manipulative and seem to love to play games. They get cozy with confrontation; they wallow in it. They destroy worlds. But, alas, I was too young and stupid to understand any of this yet.

By now my social life was so full and distracting that I was doing terrible in school. On the first grading period I got six F's and a D. I was shocked. I'd never done that bad. Luckily I was a pro at folding my report card on the grades and then inking in higher grades. I could turn a D into a C and F's into B's. My parents either didn't catch on or they played along. I suspect they played along, but either way I stayed out of trouble and promised myself I'd do better the next grading period. Louise's grades dropped too and her parents grounded her, so she couldn't hang out on weeknights at all and could only hangout on Saturday nights, on the weekend, and only after all her homework and studying were done. This did not help our relationship. It was through Louise's absence that Sam found her way in.

***

One weekend we played a house show at Hammer's house. Hammer was thirty-years-old. He'd lived in NYC and San Francisco. He'd recently moved back to Fruit Hollow to help his parents in some way. I think one of them was terminally ill or something. Anyway, you never saw them and Hammer was the first person I ever got to know who was, in a classic sense, punk-rock. He had a real mohawk, tattoos all over, and wore a leather vest and tattered jeans with cowboy boots all the time. His girlfriend, Sabrine, who was slightly younger, but still old to us, was a gorgeous tall blond who seemed to own every cool band shirt. She was super sweet to us high school kids. We were always wondering why she was with Hammer. I'm also pretty sure that Hammer was the first real alcoholic I'd ever met. He drank Popov vodka, all hours, mixed with Mountain Dew, but he never seemed drunk.

"My folks will be gone next weekend," he'd told us at the last show we'd played at The Giraffe. "I want to have a house show. Philisteens and TC are my two favorite local bands, and I want you to play." We said we'd do it. By now we had ten songs and were feeling confident and we also knew that because Hammer lived in the country right outside of Lakesburg, in an unincorporated area called Haverly, that the Lakesburg girls would be there, and probably lots of other people we'd never met before. That whole week we were psyched and we practiced three times at Josh's house just to make sure we sounded extra tight. Spencer was nearly insufferable.

"I know it's only a house show but a lot of people are going to be there and if we pull it off we might get some more gigs out of it—maybe we can play somewhere other than The giraffe and people's houses."

"Also, I've been thinking. We should take on a second guitar player. And I think it should be Garth Coffee."

Garth was a pretty cool guy. I'd known him since moving to Fruit Hollow, but, for some reason, had only really hung out with him at school. He was more of a metalhead-thrash guy and wore black all the time—all black: black jeans, black Chuck Taylor's, black t-shirts—every day. I hadn't even realized he played guitar.

"I've been to his house," said Spencer. "He has a nice guitar and a decent set up, and he really knows how to play. He's been playing all that super fast thrash shit so he should be able to pick up all our stuff no problem."

No one objected. He would be at the house show at Hammer's, just to watch us play, and he'd start practicing with us right away, if he agreed to join the band.

**

When we got to Hammer's house no one was there yet except he and Sabrine. Hammer took us to the Florida room on the far side of the house. "This is where you and TC will play. That cool?" Spencer walked around in the room, as if he was feeling out the space. He frowned and nodded. "Yeah, this'll do."

Josh laughed. "Does it have good feng shui?"

"What?"

"You're such a fucking jackass. What were you doing—feeling the vibe of the room?"

"I'm gonna kick your narrow ass," said Spencer and he jumped on Josh and they rolled around on the floor. Spencer, who was on the varsity wrestling team, put Josh in a tortuous looking hold and, with a gleeful look in his eye, said, "Do you give up?"

Josh just let out a strained giggle.

"Get off him," said Ira.

**

An hour later we had all our equipment set up, and people were starting to arrive. TC were there and they had all their equipment piled up in the corner of the Florida room where the makeshift stage would be. Josh and I were sitting on a couch close to that room and Frigg, TC's bass player, sat down next to Josh. He said nothing, just sat there. Finally Josh, feeling uncomfortable, said, "What's up?"

Frigg said, "You guys wanna smoke a joint?"

Josh looked at me and I shrugged.

"Sure," said Josh.

We ended up in the nearest bathroom and Frigg, standing next to the sink, fished around in the huge front pocket of his baggy shorts and pulled out a clear plastic baggy with several joints in it. He dug one out and lit it with a pink lighter, took a couple drags to get it going and passed it to Josh.

When we had smoked the joint down to a tiny roach, Frigg stuck out his tongue and extinguished the roach on it, looked at the roach, then popped it in his mouth, swallowed it and smiled. Josh and I chuckled. Frigg put his bag of joints back in his pocket and opened the door and walked out, closing the door behind us, leaving Josh and me in the bathroom. Following about five seconds of throbbing silence, Josh said, "Dude's a pro, man. Weird too..."

"Right?" I said, and Josh and I both seemed to have decided that the bathroom was an excellent place to hang out. Neither of us moved. We just sat there—he on the toilet and me on the edge of the tub—sighing and occasionally chuckling. After a few minutes, Ira came in, took one look at us and laughed.

"What are you two doing in here? Did I interrupt something?"

"Just smoked a joint with Frigg. Dude's weird."

Ira took his beanie cap off (he wore it no matter the weather) and unfolded one side of it and pulled out a wrinkly, bent joint. "Ready for another oner?"

"Oh Jesus," I said.

Josh made a sound like a seal barking.

Ira lit the thing and smoked about half of it before passing it to me. I took a hit and handed it over to Josh. Josh held it up to his eyes and stared at it for what seemed like minutes. Ira slapped him on the ear. Josh jolted, like he was coming out of a trance, and then looked over at Ira.

"Smoke it or pass it," he said.

Josh took an awkward hit of it and then, weaving it, passed it to me.

When we were done, Ira gently tamped the roach out in the sink, rinsed the sink out, and put the roach back in the fold of his beanie cap.

"Good night, boys," he said on his way out.

Josh and I were alone again.

"I don't know what to do," I said.

Josh looked down at his open palms. "Me neither," he whispered.

A moment later the door opened again, and it was a pretty girl, one of the Lakesburg girls, tall and lanky, bobbed black hair, named Tracy. She smiled at both of us, pointed at me, giggled, and said, "Get out of here, you two." We obeyed and walked into the hall and then out into the main living room where there were now maybe fifty people milling around and talking in groups, drinking, smoking, laughing, shrieking, and we both stood there stunned. Josh saw a person he knew, someone, I presume, who didn't scare him in his present state of heightened awareness, and I was left there feeling alone. I saw Ira and Spencer in the Florida room. Ira was tuning up and Spencer was doing something with the microphone.

I walked up to Ira and stood next to him. Spencer glanced over at me and went back to what he was doing. "Garth should be here soon," he said. "We'll start when he gets here."

***

Josh, our drummer, and I, our bass player, were so trashed that we sounded like pure shit that night. You can't have your rhythm section be off and sound any good. You can get by with a drunk or high guitar player, but not your rhythm section. Ira thought it was funny, but Spencer, the professional, was pissed, he didn't talk to me or Josh for a week. Garth, who'd come to hear us to decide if he wanted to be in our band, didn't mind.

"Hey, man. I just want to have some fun," he'd said, after we played. We all stayed and watched TC, of course, and they sounded amazing, as usual. The Lakesburg girls were there, too, but I was too out of it to talk to any of them and went home early. Dude, who was becoming our most loyal fan and now had an old beater Honda Civic, elected to drive me home, as my house was on the way.

After the week of silence, Spencer made me promise never to get trashed before a show. "I don't care what you do after we play," he said. "The only reason I don't throw you out for some other mediocre bass player is because I like you. And the only other person I know who plays bass and has equipment, and is available, is that bird faced asshat, Andre."

Five

A COUPLE OF WEEKS AFTER HAMMER'S house-show Louise blind-sided me. She stopped by Josh's house while we were practicing and waited for us to finish the song we'd been playing when she walked in.

"I can't talk," she said, and she held out her hand, wherein she held paper folded into a diamond shape.

"A note?"

She smiled and caressed my shoulder. She waved at the band and walked out.

The note read as follows:

Neil,

I don't know how to say this except just to say it: things aren't working out. You're really nice, and I like you but, to be honest, I like someone else. I hope we can still be friends, because I really do think of you as a friend. We can talk about this later, if you want to, but I had to get it out. I had to let you know, because it was killing me, and I knew we wouldn't have a chance to talk any time soon.

I'm sorry.
Louise.

Louise was my first girlfriend and the first girl I might have loved. I went into Josh's hall bathroom and just sat in there for a few minutes. I heard the band playing our newest song without me. I felt numb and my face was hot. I thought about every girl I've ever liked or felt anything for. I thought about Natatie and Hillary, and even Heather, my perverse babysitter. I thought about Sam, too, which made me feel a little better. I thought about her saying, "Let me know when you no longer have a girlfriend." I got so focused I forgot where I was until I heard someone whistle from the other side of the bathroom door.

"Neil?" a voice said.

"Uh, yeah?"

"You okay?"

I walked out of the bathroom and saw tall, lanky Garth Coffee standing there with a huge grin full of braces.

He pulled from his t-shirt pocket a red pack of cigarettes.

"Want one?"

I didn't really smoke, but, I figured, what the hell.

We stood in Josh's front yard and smoked and talked and Garth said he was stoked about joining the band.

"Spencer's kind of a dick, but we have fun. It's cool to have you in the band."

He finished his cigarette and flicked the butt into the gutter.

"Better get back in there…"

I flicked my butt into the gutter too and we both walked back into the house and into the garage.

I thought about Louise some more, and then I thought about Sam again, the blond Lakesburg girl who talked like an actress. I was beginning to feel better.

***

Spencer had been right. A guy who booked shows for this small new-wave dance club in Lakesburg had seen us play at Hammer's and, despite our sloppiness, liked us. He asked us to open for this reggae / ska band called Inspektor-12, and we'd agreed—or Spencer had agreed. He'd asked him at the end of the night, and he was the only sober one in the band.

"A reggae band?" I'd asked. "A punk band opening for a reggae band?"

"They're more of a ska band. I've seen them before. They're pretty cool. It'll be good exposure."

***

The club was called The Undergound. I'd never been there, but I'd heard of it and I knew that some big, out of town bands had played there. We were all game. And this would be our first show with Garth in the band, as second guitar. We practiced three times a week for three weeks, and Garth was a quick study. He learned all our songs and even contributed some back-up vocals.

***

When we arrived, Inspektor-12 was already there. They had a truck and an enclosed trailer with stickers all over it where they kept their equipment. They looked like a real touring band. Two of the band members, the drummer and the singer, were standing out front smoking cigarettes and talking to a group of girls I didn't recognize.

"Shit," said Ira. "This is awesome. It's like a real gig."

We pulled around back and then walked around front and approached the group talking and smoking. The drummer of I-12 was tall and lanky and had dreadlocks down his back. The singer was a black guy dressed in a black suit and wearing a porkpie hat. He was also wearing super dark sunglasses.

"What's up?" said Spencer. "We're the opening band."

Neither said anything, but the drummer held out his hand and Spencer took it and the singer said, "Let's go inside." The group of girls went off to the side and started whispering and giggling, except for one, a girl dressed like a skinhead. She had a Chelsea Girl haircut and wore oxblood doc martens and a green bomber jacket. She was staring at Spencer. Garth came up behind me and dropped an elbow on my back and screeched. I turned around and jumped on him and put him in a headlock. He spun me around and the girls laughed.

"Cut the shit," said Spencer.

We all went inside and Spencer and the two I-12 guys walked up to the stage and talked and pointed at shit.

***

The show went well. We sounded tight and Garth did great and when we were done playing Garth and Ira and I went out back. Spencer stayed inside and watched I-12. Garth lit up a cigarette and offered me one. I took it and we stood with Ira and talked about how great the show was. After a few minutes the group of girls from before the show walked up and the skinhead girl said hi.

"I've got a van in the back of the lot and a cooler full of beer. You guys wanna come hang for a bit?"

We just looked at her.

"Come on," she said, and we followed her.

It was a full-size black van and when she opened the side door smoke rolled out and we could see the rest of the girls, all with quarts of beer in hand, and one had a bong at her feet. We stepped in and the Chelsea girl took the driver seat and we just filled in the empty spaces in the back. A girl in tight jeans, a plain black pocket tee, and low-top chucks, handed us quarts of Old English 800. Another girl, one dressed in a flowing hippy dress, picked up the bong and put a lighter to the bowl.

"You guys sounded great," said the one in tight jeans.

"Where y'all from?" said Ira.

"Tampa," said tight jeans. "My names Krystal. That's Gilly and that's Reese." Reese was the skinhead girl.

"Can I hit that bong?" said Ira. Gilly handed it over and Garth chuckled.

We all sat and smoked and drank and listened to some ska band I'd never heard before, but it was all good and everything felt cool and right.

"We came with Inspektor-12," Reese finally said. "I guess we're groupies."

They all laughed a little too hard, and I felt uncomfortable for the first time.

"You guys in high school," said gilly with a silly grin.

"Yeah," I said. 'What about you?"

"Dropped out," said Gilly.

"I'm home-schooled said Reese."

Krystal just smiled.

"You're cute," said Gilly, looking at me. She stood up and took her shirt off. She wasn't wearing a bra.

"Oh, shit!" said Garth.

Ira busted out laughing.

Krystal stood up and gave Gilly a kiss and grabbed her breast.

I'd like to say here that we all hunkered down and took advantage of the situation, but we didn't. We all, almost simultaneously, stood up and Garth said, "I guess we should get back." We didn't even bring our quarts of beer with us. I grabbed the door handle and opened up the door and we all stumbled out. We laughed and giggled all the way back to the front entrance to the club. Chicken shit high school kids.

Ira went inside and Garth and I stayed out front and talked to TC who had showed up late and were hanging out front talking to people.

"We just met a girl with your name," I said to Reese.

"A skinhead chic? I know here," he said.

"Seems like you already know every girl I meet," I said, feeling bold from the beer.

He smiled wryly.

Garth came up behind me and put me in a full nelson. I struggled and somehow managed to twist him around and get him in a headlock, and he hoisted me up and drove me into a huge old-style marquee window next to the entrance to the club, which used to be a movie theater. The window came crashing down on us and we fell into it.

I opened my eyes and Garth was standing over me with his hand out. I took his hand and he hoisted me up. Stunned, I looked at my arms and body to see if I was okay. Bits of glass were all over me and in my hair, but I didn't seem to be bleeding, and neither did Garth. Once we both realized we were okay we started laughing. Reese shook his head and smiled. We both realized a small, prematurely balding man, dressed in a paisley button up and tight black jeans was staring at us.

"This is unbelievable…" he said.

A crowd had gathered. The girls from the van and other onlookers had encircled us. Spencer and Ira were close by.

"Fucking high-school punk rock shits. I should have known better."

I looked over at Spencer, who I assumed was pissed with Garth and me. He did look pissed, but he was glaring at the little club owner.

"Your club," said Spencer, "is a shithole. We're the coolest fucking band you've ever had play here. And don't think you're not paying us because of this." He moved closer to him, and the little man darted away, into his club, with a squeal.

Spencer turned to me and Garth. "You fucking assholes…" he said and walked away.

I shrugged and looked around. Most of the people were smiling. Gilly, the girl who'd exposed herself in the van, was looking particularly fetching. Reese, from Transmission Cancelled, walked up to me and Garth.

"Dude," he said, "that was fucking punk."

Six

SUMMER ENDED AND WE ALL unceremoniously went back to school. Well, not all of us. Garth decided school was for chumps and just quit going. So did a few others, peripheral members of our clique. None of us were scholars—except maybe Spencer. It got me thinking, too. School sucked and by the halfway point of junior year I was barely passing. I ran the idea of quitting school by my dad and got a seriously rude awakening. We were driving somewhere—to Corley and Twyla's, I think. In the muffled quiet of the pick-up cab I broached the subject.

"I been thinking," I said.

Dad hummed an um-hm.

"School sucks and I'm barely passing and—you know—a bunch of guys I know have dropped out and are going to adult school—finishing up their high school diploma at night. I think I could do something like that. They get it done quicker that way, too. Save some time. Staying in school's just a waste of time... seems like."

Dad nudged the blinker lever and it click-clacked until he completed the turn onto Corley and Twyla's street.

"Tell you what," he said, paused.

Oh shit, I thought.

He applied the breaks and pulled onto the side of the road, about half a block from Corley and Twyla's.

"You can do that. You can do anything you want, right? But if you do, there will be repercussions..."

"Mom..." I said.

"Well, yeah. It would break her heart. But that's not what I'm talking about. Did you know that I wanted to drop out of high school?"

I did not respond. He looked over at me and I looked at him. I could sense a story looming.

"I was a senior and it was the beginning of the year. I was fed up—like you—and a few of my friends had quit already. I told my mama I was gonna quit. She said, 'I wish you wouldn't.' That's all she said. I told her, tough shit and walked out the house, like a big man. That Saturday Uncle Lonny and Leland came by the house early, got me out of bed, and told me to hurry up and get dressed and meet them outside... They sat in Lonny's yellow Dodge pick-up and when I walked out Lonny told me to jump in the back. Long story short, they took me out into the woods—out offa Croom's Road—deep into the scrub oaks and pines and they beat the tar out of me..." He paused. "I mean they beat the living shit out of me and they never did mention school or mama or nothing—just beat me until I couldn't move and drove my sorry ass home and carried me into my room and dropped me on the bed and left. I'll never forget the sound of Lonny's Dodge pulling out of the gravel driveway. For some reason that really stands out."

"Jesus," I said. "That's harsh."

"Made A's and B's the rest of the year and graduated with honors."

He pulled back onto the road, without saying another word, and drove the rest of the way to Corley and Twyla's in silence.

Message received. I never again brought up the idea of dropping out of school.

***

I didn't graduate with honors, but I did get my shit together and passed all my classes that year. The implication had been clear. An ass beating lay in wait if I didn't graduate high school.

***

By the end of junior year, we'd played about ten more shows and had gotten tight as a band. Garth had blended in well, and added some real dimension to the band. He had a cool grungy look and had a good chunky, rusty guitar sound that contrasted nicely with Ira's thinner, staticky sound. Our tastes had broadened, and we had written a few more songs, and we were less of a straight ahead punk band and more of a noise band. We'd retooled our older songs to match this new aesthetic. Spencer had discovered Big Black and Drive Like Jehu and we had all gotten into Fugazi and Jawbox, so we, naturally, wanted to sound like all those bands. We didn't, but we tried.

Spencer and I had had a serious talk one weekend the last month of our junior year. We'd come to the realization that the summer before our senior year could conceivably be our last hurrah as a band. "We probably have this summer, and maybe a few gigs during our senior year, and then once we all graduate, we'll probably be doing our own separate things. We need to make this summer count. Play as many shows as we can. Maybe even do a little mini-tour—play in Tampa, Orlando, Melbourne, and some other places maybe."

I agreed. And we set to convincing the rest of the band, which wasn't hard. Josh was up for whatever. Ira said he had to figure out how to get out of a family summer trip, but if he couldn't we still had Garth. We could get by with one guitar player.

***

It was like Louise and I had never dated. We'd see each other in the halls and nod or smile or wave but that's about it. She'd started dating this cross-country dude, a tall, skinny guy named Condon, who was into poetry, of all the things. He was like no one I'd ever met, which was his appeal to Louise, I'm sure. She had a real thing for novelty. She was always calling things 'neat' that weren't really that neat, just out-of-the-ordinary. This Condon dude could sometimes be seen (and heard) walking down the hallways at school reciting poetry. I didn't know how he got away with that. I would have gotten my ass beat for doing something like that. But this Condon guy, all of six foot four, and lanky as hell, wearing his cross-country letterman jacket, could do it, and either you just ignored him or laughed at him. He didn't care and no one else really seemed to either. I guess that's what Louise, and most other girls at school, saw in him. He didn't give a shit. He liked what he liked and did whatever he wanted to. He was an eccentric. Me and my friends thought we were, but he really was. We were just another clique at school. You had jocks, stoners, hicks, gangsters, nerds, and you had us. We were usually refered to by those others groups as 'freaks,' but we were punks, skaters, goths, new wavers...basically all the music-centered groups. Condon was a clique of one—two, really, now that he and Louise were together.

Unfortunately, I'd lost track of Sam too. She'd quit coming to shows. Word was she had gotten super into academics, had decided she wanted to get into Harvard or some such place, and was taking some kind of summer dual-enrolment classes at an IB school in Orlando. This was a bit disheartening for me. I'd thought for sure we would end up together, at least for a while.

As for Philisteens, we were doing what we'd sat out to do for the summer. Spencer had started actually booking shows so by the time summer rolled around we had an itinerary, a tour schedule. We had shows booked, on a rolling basis at the three clubs in the county who would have us, and we had a few shows booked in Orlando, and a few in Tampa, and one in Melbourne, a two-hour drive from Fruit Hollow, pretty far afield for us.

Dad had lost his job at the fire department and worked unloading trucks at some shipping company now. Mom had had to find a job to help take up the slack, and she'd ended up at a citrus packing warehouse, called Hunt's Citrus. Things were tough. Money was tight. I was fine, had one academic year left and I'd be out, but I felt bad for brother-man. He was only nine-going-on-ten, and was somewhat helpless. I tried to give him a couple bucks, here and there, but I didn't have much money, myself. Once I'd earned enough to pay off my music equipment, I quit my job with Paul. I hated working. I hated being somewhere I didn't want to be. Work was bullshit. I hated it so much that I could seriously put myself into a deep depression if I thought too hard and long on what would happen after graduation. I wasn't a good student, and I had no tangible interests, beyond playing music and skateboarding, neither of which I was good enough at to make any money doing. I was probably screwed. I'd graduate and do yard work or restaurant work for a living. Shit work. Work no one wanted to do. Alternatives? Join the military... No thanks.

Seven

DAD'S LOSING HIS JOB WITH THE FIRE department didn't exactly thrill my mom. She was working now, and she hated working as much as I did—maybe more. So they fought a lot when they were home together, which, mercifully, wasn't that often. Dad was working seventy and eighty hours a week and mom was working thirty. James and I weren't used to this. We weren't latch-key kids. We were used to coming home to meals and a kitchen pantry full of food, and a fridge full of leftovers and things to drink. We were mostly on our own now, and, while I enjoyed the freedom, the situation was tough for James.

***

The thing is, Dad didn't seem to give a shit. He worked just as hard at this shit job as he had as a firefighter. Anytime I tried to find out what had happened, why he wasn't a firefighter anymore, he'd just say something like, "It's just a bunch of bullshit. I don't wanna get into it…"

And I'd say, "Yeah, a bunch of bullshit…"

And he'd tell me not to cuss, and we'd go about our business.

For some reason I couldn't ask Mom. The thought of asking her about it scared me. I didn't like to ask her serious things.

Many years later, I would learn something of what happened to my father. I had moved back to the beach for a little while in my mid-twenties and, one night, had gone out to eat at a place we used to go to all the time when I was a kid—a raw bar my parents had loved. I ran into one of my dad's old buddies, who had also been a firefighter—still was. He called me over and I ended up having dinner with he and his wife, and we drank a couple pitchers of beer, and he just came out with it. I'm sure he assumed I knew. I'm sure he didn't think he was telling me anything new.

"I sure do wish your dad coulda got his act together and took things a little more seriously. He was the best firefighter I knew. I mean, in certain ways, he was the best." He paused and looked over my shoulder, as if watching a little movie that was playing there. "I seen your dad do shit no one else would do. I seen that fat fuck roll under a burning airplane. I seen him jump into the broken window of a burning house to fetch a lady's 'baby,' a fucking rat terrier. He was so good in a crisis. Could think on his feet like no one else. But, gaddamn…" He paused and took a good swig of beer. "Sonofabitch couldn't take getting passed over for chief, and couldn't take a lesser man telling him what to do. Too full of pride, your dad."

I just grimaced and shook my head.

"You know what I mean…" he said, and I couldn't

tell if it was a question or a statement. I didn't ask for further explanation. I knew enough, and understood enough. It added up. It all sounded like my dad.

***

The Philisteens had a reputation now as a crazy punk-noise band who were unpredictable and, as people liked to say, authentic—whatever that meant. We were an unkindness of high school punk bastards. We broke shit and got drunk with your girlfriend. Raw talent. Raw energy. Raw everything. You want a bunch of misfit bastard children to show up to your gig? Book Philisteens. This was, of course, a good and a bad thing. We had fun, but there was no guarantee you were going to. We started to like the image we were given a little too much. We got a kick out of becoming what people thought we already were. It was, for some of us, too much to live up to.

That summer, Ira, Josh, Garth and I took things to a new level. If we'd known the word *debauchery* we'd have gladly—gleefully—declared that summer The Summer of Our Debauchery. We quite rapidly became a glaring of little degenerates.

***

Orlando was cool, but Tampa was the best—our favorite, hands down. Especially Cuba Town, with its crumbling-red-brick, old-world, criminal charm. There was even actual, real organized crime in the little enclave. The Cuban mafia. There was a restaurant, La Tropical, on the main strip, Seventh Ave, that, seemingly, was never opened to the public, but there were always people inside—old men, smoking cigars and sitting around a table. They fascinated us endlessly. Garth and I liked to stare through the windows. The men inside didn't even acknowledge us. They were, I'm sure, used to it.

It was an anything goes kind of place, Cuba Town. As long as you didn't look twelve you could drink at any bar or club and there were artists and writers and punks and hippies and beatniks and all other manner of misfit folk there. No one gave a shit what you did, as long as you kept your cool, and there were always great bands playing, any night of the week, and there was a used record store, and beautiful young ladies all over the place, and all of it, on an eight block span of one road. You could walk everywhere you wanted to go. For all of these reasons, it had Orlando beat. Orlando was too spread out and—worse—Olrando was home to Magic Kingdom and Sea World and Wet 'N' Wild and all those other really square, bullshit family places that, for most of us, our own families couldn't afford to take us to. Tampa had Busch Gardens, but Busch Gardens was a grungier Florida 'attraction,' and it was owned by a brewery—albeit the biggest brewery in the world—but still… Tampa, and Cuba Town, specifically, was a kind of oasis for wayward young Floridians. It seemed, in those days, you never saw anyone over the age of twenty-five in Cuba Town, except for the old Cuban Mafiosi, so we played as many shows there as we could, which wasn't actually that many, because Tampa had so many of its own cool bands that we were just white noise, really. We were high school grommets from the sticks, from the boonies and weren't that well connected. But we got lucky enough to play a few shows in Cuba Town that summer between eleventh and twelfth grade. In addition, we hung out there as much as possible.

***

Ira's grandmother lived in Tampa, about a ten-minute drive

from Cuba Town and she was always happy to let us crash there. Her house was a typical old-school Florida home from the forties or fifties: brick and block, flat tar roof, and a tiny one-car garage. At some point, Ira's granddad, dead now, had converted the garage into an office. It was now an extra room with its own door to the outside and Ira's grandmother, Sophia, had given Ira a key to that side-door. She'd told him that whenever he was in town he could use the room, and if he came in late at night, to just use the key to come in the side-door. She didn't care. Hell, most of the time she'd make us breakfast. She'd open the inside door and peak in at us crashed out all over the room. Within minutes you'd smell bacon or sausage frying and coffee percolating. It was great.

Sophia was funny too. She was an old Russian lady, and was very suspicious of the Cubans, whom she referred to as "Latins." She called me something that in Russian meant "shitty pants," because I always wore baggy pants, and it sounded like, "shranny pants." She never once called me by my name, but she was sweet to me, treated me like she may have thought I was an orphan, or just a victim of vague but serious misfortunes.

Sophia also made us potato pancakes and piroshki and other Russian food. We had a great time at Sophia's place, but it was also very sad. I hated to leave her. I pictured her piddling around in her kitchen putting away leftovers and then sitting in her empty living room all alone watching TV and waiting for the next time we'd come visit so she could make us piroshki and sweet tea.

***

One of these times we opened for a band at this little shithole club in Cuba Town called Comet Club. It was a little bigger than a two-car garage. It had no ac, no stage and there was a five-dollar cover, for three bands—us, a droning Flipper-like band called Pulse and a band called Fuckface who wore ski masks and sang about robbing banks. It was a packed house. There was a 'bar' of sorts at the Comet Club. The owner had one of those folding cafeteria tables he stood behind with a huge cooler full of PBR and Busch Lite he sold for a dollar a can. No ID's were checked, of course, and I was pretty sure there were some fourteen-year-olds drinking in there.

We opened, and the response was decent. People danced and everyone seemed to be having a good time. Fuckface was next and they really got the crowd going. The singer was wild and you could see spit flying out of the mouth of his balaclava and he jumped and gyrated. Three songs in, he had taken his shirt off, and ripped handfuls of chest hair out and threw them into the audience. His voice was rough, course and angry. He even had an endless supply of PBR being handed to him by a cute redhead stage left. Their set lasted about forty-five minutes, and when they walked off stage, the small cave like club was so hot everyone was sticky with sweat and the atmosphere was dank and humid. I had to walk outside to get some air, but it wasn't much different. July in central Florida is hot and humid most of the time.

As I walked back inside a kid, maybe fifteen-years-old, vomited and I got a little splash on my low top Chucks.

"Fuck, man!" The poor kid was on his side, curled up, and two gutter punks were laughing at him. A young lady in a Minor Threat shirt was yelling at the gutter punks and almost crying. The gist was that the vomiter was her little brother and they'd been feeding him beers, gotten him wrecked for the fun of it.

I tapped her on the shoulder and yelled into her ear. "You want me to help you drag him off somewhere!"

She gave me a look over and then nodded.

We each took an arm and dragged him to the side of the building. To my surprise there was a little breeze, and there was a tall palm tree, with long dried out fronds that hissed in the wind. It was a different world on this side of the building and we propped the kid up against the wall.

"Dude's trashed…"

"His name's Scott. He's my dumbass brother. Only thirteen."

I couldn't believe he was only thirteen. Poor kid.

"Those older guys get him like this?"

"Yeah, those older guys are fucking assholes. They just graduated from high school last year. I know them from school."

"My name's Neil by the way."

"Jessie," she said with a wave. "Which school do you go to?"

"Oh, I'm from Fruit Hollow, so you wouldn't know the school. I'll be a senior next year, though."

"Me too," she said. She pulled a pack of generic cigarettes from her back jeans pocket and lit one. She pointed the pack and lighter at me.

I took the pack and lit one.

"Thanks for helping. My car's out back. Hopefully he'll be able to walk by then… Hey," she said with a tilt of her head. "Were you in the opening band?"

"Yeah, I'm the bass player."

"I really liked you guys," she said.

I thanked her, sat down next to her inebriated brother and leaned against the wall. "If you need help getting him to the car later, I can stick around."

She smiled. "Maybe," she said. She threw down her cigarette butt and stepped on it. Her brother moaned and turned to his side and laid his back against the wall. He mumbled something that sounded like, *that's better…*

We both laughed.

The tempo and volume of the music coming from inside changed and we both took a few seconds to listen.

"Shit," she said. "Pulse. They're why I came here. They're my favorite central Florida band."

I stood up, looked down at her brother. "Well, let's carry him to your car, put him in the back seat, crack the window, and lock him in. He'll be fine. Then we can go watch Pulse."

I could tell she was almost sold on the idea—but not quite. "No, I can't. If anything happened to him I'd be in deep shit. I'd never get to go anywhere again. Yeah, I think the night's over for us. Help me get him to the car, and we'll take off. But thanks for the offer."

***

After we loaded the little shit into the car, I saw Jessie to the driver's side and she got on her toes and gave me a kiss on the cheek, and I did something I'd never done before. I asked her for her number. She found an empty cigarette pack on the floorboard and tore off a piece and wrote her number on it and handed it to me.

"Do you drive?" she said.

"Well, yeah. But I don't have a car."

She put her hand to her chin and seemed to be thinking about things.

"My dad lets me borrow his truck sometimes, though. Plus we have a couple more shows around here soon."

She smiled and said goodnight. Her brother propped himself up and looked around with bleary eyes.

"What the fuck," he said. "Who's this guy?"

"Lie down, jackass," said Jessie and he complied.

Eight

SUMMER FLEW BY. WE PLAYED OUR SHOWS and spent a lot of time in Tampa and Cuba Town, and at the end of summer we went back to school. We played a few weekend shows throughout the school year, but we all seemed to be moving in different directions, as Spencer had predicted. We started making plans for the next summer, for our post-graduation lives. A few friends of mine applied to colleges, a few applied to community college, but Garth and I had no plans for higher education. I had no plans at all. I truly had no idea what to do after graduation.

I'd been seeing Jessie for a few months now and moving to Tampa was the closest thing to an idea I had, but it started and stopped there. What would I do in Tampa? Where would I work? I had no discernible skills. I was a lousy bass player. I had done some landscaping work, but was scared out of my mind of snakes and spiders.

Garth had already dropped out of school and had a job as a line cook at a Village Inn and I spent many afternoons, after school, at his apartment, which was two blocks away from the school in what, to me, seemed like a really nice apartment complex. At first, I wasn't sure how he could afford it on a line cook's salary, but later I found out that his dad, who had always seemed like a real hard-ass, said if you're going to drop out of school you're not going to live under my roof, and was actually paying half his rent so that he could afford a decent place, instead of some slum.

I spent a lot of time at Garth's, even if he wasn't there, hanging out and watching movies or listening to music or smoking pot with Garth's unofficial roommate, a guy named Clive who was twenty-six and had no apparent aspirations in life beyond smoking copious amounts of pot and working at the multiplex movie theatre in town. Pot and movies. His life. To be fair, his knowledge of the film industry was impressive. He was like a full professor of film. And he'd let us into movies for free. He was an assistant manager at the Draft House Multiplex and, if he was working, and the manager wasn't, he'd let us in to see whatever we wanted. *Carlito's Way, True Romance, Falling Down, In the Name of The Father, Benny & Joon, So I Married an Axe Murderer,* Coppola's *Dracula, Alien 3,* and so on. We saw so many movies, good and shitty. It didn't matter. Admission was free. We'd usually get high first, and, of course, we'd bring in contraband, cheap snacks and drinks, instead of the expensive stuff they sold at concessions.

Something interesting and vaguely unsettling began to happen. I didn't quite get why, or what exactly it was, but all that mattered to me, all that I really noticed, was that my social group was splintering. When I started hanging out a lot at Garth's, Spencer started hanging out with people I'd never seen him hang out with before, preps and geeks—the collegebound kids. And all the really talented musicians started hanging out with Reese. It seemed to me that a further sorting out was happening, and I noticed quite clearly what group I was in. I was in the flunky group. All the people who I found myself hanging around when we weren't practicing were the stoners, druggies, dropouts, losers. The shiftless bunch. I found this disconcerting. But I didn't dwell on it. If it was my lot, so be it.

***

One day, towards the end of the school year, I was sitting on Garth's couch after school and there was a knocked at the door. I was the only one there, and I got up and looked through the peephole on the door and it was Spencer, who never came over to Garth's. Other than band practice, I never saw the two of them together. I, it must be said, had just finished smoking a joint all by myself and was super paranoid. I just stood there looking through the peephole at Spencer. He knocked again. I kept staring. I felt like I wasn't breathing. He pulled his backpack around, got out a pen and a sheet of paper and started to write. He wrote on it for a while. He filled one whole side of the page. He folded it in half. Then he looked right at me—or seemed to—and flicked off the peephole. "I know you're in there, fucker," he said. Then he bent down and slid the paper under the door and walked away. I watched him until he disappeared. My heart was pounding. I felt like I might get sick. I looked down at the folded paper at my feet.

Neil,
First of all—you're a goddamn idiot…But I'm worried about you.
All you do is hang out here at Garth's house, and did you know that
Garth is an idiot too—an actual idiot. (You're not actually an idiot;

you're just acting like one.) I get it. He's a nice guy, and seems fun to be around. But, really, he's just a total goddamn motherfucking idiot. He's going nowhere and doing nothing and you're going nowhere and doing nothing with him. We—you and I—used to be friends, man. What happened? Is it just that I'm not dumb enough? Do I make things too hard? Anyway, I just wanted to tell you that you are better than this shit—just going to practice—skipping school all the time— and hanging at the den of dunces, smoking pot and drinking. You are who you associate with. That's a fact, man. And you're turning into one of these stoner dicks who sit around and watch TV and get high all day.

Remember skateboarding?

Remember being into music?

Remember being into anything?

That's all. I hope I see you at practice. Oh, that's the other thing—if you practiced at all you'd be an amazing bass player, instead of just a mediocre one.

Later bitch…

I wanted to chase Spencer down and grab him by the shoulder and turn him around and straighten him out on some shit, but he was right. He was already straight on shit. I was the one who needed straightening. I knew that. I cared what he thought. Also, and I didn't think of this at the time, but I was touched, as well. I couldn't believe that he'd cared enough to take the time to call me out, to confront me. It was brave and it was compassionate, even if it lacked a bit in the tact department. But maybe the time for tact was over. Maybe he had already been tactful and I hadn't noticed. I sat there on Garth's couch, the TV blaring some nonsense, and I cried. I cried for a while. And when I was done crying, I walked into the kitchen and put the note in the sink and burned it. I never went to band practice again and never spoke to Spencer again.

***

That summer, about a week after graduation, I moved in with Garth. I'd got a job washing dishes at a little Italian restaurant called Gino's a few weeks before school let out for the summer. I didn't make much—about a hundred and fifty a week—but I didn't need much. Garth's dad quit paying half the rent when he found out he had another room-mate, but it was fine. Clive was official now too, so we split the rent three ways. Garth paid all the utilities, though, because he had the master bedroom with his own bathroom and Clive and I shared a bedroom and the hall bathroom. Living there, though, was different. Now that I was there full-time it changed things.

My parents seemed okay with all this. They hadn't ever expected much from me. The day I left, though, my mom cried, and James seemed a little upset too. Dad just said, "If you ever need anything, or if you get in trouble, let me know. I'll do whatever I can to help." I thanked him. Garth was sitting in his truck in the driveway waiting. The bed of the truck was loaded with my things. "Here," said Dad. He handed me some folded bills. "It's not much, but it should help you out a little with things." We all hugged and I left, got in the truck with Garth, and we drove home.

If I wasn't at work I was home—at our place. I didn't make enough money to go anywhere. I started to see a different side of the place. Before, when I got tired or bored, I could go home. I could leave the party atmosphere. Not anymore. Now I was stuck there. It didn't take long for me to hate it there.

***

I was no longer in the band and neither was Garth (when he found out I quit, so did he) and they, I learned through word of mouth, had morphed into a new band, with Reese from TC and a couple guys from a popular grindcore band from Tampa called Shite. They were good, I'd heard—really good. They were super heavy and slow and sounded, I was told, like a talented Flipper. Their new name was Petrichor.

One weekend, I found out they'd be playing a show at a small club in Tampa called SLAM. Garth and I decided we'd go, see what they were like. We had no hard feelings toward them and they were still, technically, our friends, and there would be other people there who we wanted to see. I called Jessie to see if she wanted to meet up there and she said she had been planning to go anyway because a friend of hers was the singer of the main act, a band called Talon, who was a crazy screamo band that was renowned for their highly idiosyncratic and high energy performances.

It was a great show. Petrichor was great. They had great presence. They all affected this tired, exasperated look, and moved in unison. And they were loud and heavy—the loudest band I'd ever heard. Talon was the best live band I'd seen up to that point. I looked all over for Spencer and Josh and Reese after the show but couldn't find them for the longest time. Finally I saw Spencer, around back of SLAM, talking to a man I knew to be the owner of the club. I walked up to them and Spencer looked at me, smiled, and went back to talking to the club owner. I waited a few minutes for them to stop talking, for Spencer to acknowledge me, but it wasn't happening, so I turned and walked away. I thought maybe Spencer might stop me, or call my name and catch up with me, but he never did.

After the show Garth and I hung out with Jessie and Smitty, the singer of Talon, who was a pretty quiet guy.

Smitty was nineteen and had his own house in

Tampa—not an apartment, but an entire house. I'd never met a young person about my age with a house before. It was a rundown shotgun shack painted purple on the outside. The living room was pink and he had a hodge-podge of furniture and actual original art on the walls, and the art was by people he knew. Smitty, Jessie, Garth and I had stopped at a Jamaica-themed convenience store that also sold jerk chicken and got two cases of Red Stripe on the way and by the time we got to Smitty's place there were already ten or so people in his house. When he saw the perplexed look on my face, Smitty said, "I don't lock the door. Friends know they can come in whenever they want to. It's not a big deal…"

We drank beer and smoked pot and listened to records—mostly bands I'd never heard of. Garth, Jessie and I ended up sleeping on the floor, like hobos, and when we woke up, there were people all over the house, sleeping or just waking up. Smitty was cooking eggs and bacon, and a vegan guy was haranguing him.

Garth and I walked onto the front porch and shared a cigarette.

"I gotta go soon. I have to work tomorrow."

Jessie walked out and lit a cigarette.

"Looks like we'll be heading out soon."

She leaned against the porch railing.

"Can't you stay till tomorrow. There's supposed to be a big private party downtown at this microbrewery. It's free and I know the owner's son so underage drinking is a sure thing."

I looked at Garth.

"Sounds great, but I can't."

"Why can't you stay?"

"I guess I can. But how will I get home Sunday. I've got work Monday. I can't miss work."

"I'll drive you home, it's only an hour and a half

round trip. As for work—fuck it."

    So I stayed—and not just for the weekend.

Nine

STAYED WITH SMITTY FOR A MONTH. JESSIE AND
I took a couple trips back to Garth's so I could get my
things, and I stored what few possessions I had in
Smitty's attic and rode the couch. In the meantime Jessie
and I fixed up an efficiency her mother owned in Sawpalm
Beach: the small bayside community they lived in. It was an
older neighborhood, all the homes had been built in the
twenties and thirties. Parts of it were shabby but nice, had
been kept up and had an old-Florida charm; other parts were
just run down and shitty. Our prospective place was in the
latter category. If we fixed it up, she said, we could stay there
for one-fifty a month for as long as we liked. The place
needed painting and just a general cleaning up. It hadn't been
inhabited for over a year. We also had to replace a window
in the bathroom that had been cracked during a tropical
storm.

      The place was great for us. It was situated across the

street from a seawall where we could sit and watch the tide come in and go out.

Jessie's mother, Janice, it turned out, was very liberal about things concerning her daughter. She seemed cool to me, and during the time we spent fixing up the place on the bay we would often spend evenings at her place drinking beer and laughing and planning for the future.

Before long Jessie and I had fixed up and moved into the new place. By then I had a job washing dishes at a New Orleans-themed barbeque place called Gumbo's. I worked thirty hours a week and didn't make much money, but I didn't need much money, and when I wasn't at work I didn't do much except go to punk shows with Jessie and drink beer. Jessie made more money. She waited tables at a more upscale place downtown, a restaurant inside a big, fancy hotel where business-people stayed and they were serious over-tippers. Jessie was cute so she took full advantage of the situation. Things were fine. Better than fine. We were surviving. We worked, we paid our bills and we had a little money to have fun.

But when I was alone, I felt hollow. Usually this happened when I was at work. I knew no one there and I kept my head down and did my job, washed dishes. The hours went by and I had nothing to do but think. I thought about Fruit Hollow a lot, about James and mom and dad and my friends who were still there, and friends who weren't. I thought about friends who moved elsewhere. I found it odd that I was the only one who'd found his way to Tampa and to Cuba Town. We'd all come here and we'd all, more or less, loved it. I had anticipated—or would have had I the foresight to anticipate—that more of us would have made it out here. I was lonely, but it seemed to me that that was just the way it was. When you graduated from high school and moved to a different city, even one that was only a short drive away, you felt lonely and a little sad. Plus I still didn't have a car so I couldn't go visit people in Fruit Hollow. It felt like much farther away than it was. I felt like I was in another state, or on a remote island.

But when Jessie and I were together I almost never felt this way, and Smitty was becoming one of my best friends, and Garth, who was now selling drugs (weed, ecstasy and acid, mostly), came as often as possible to visit. He started to use our place as a 'base' for his sales. No drug deals went down at our small apartment, but he would stay with us and set up deals at nearby places using the payphone at the Jiffy two blocks away from our place.

Jessie and I had been living together for a year, and things were not bad, but I could sense a subtle shift. I was working at a place called Cuba Town Pizza now. It was a little punk place where you could get a slice of cheese pizza for a buck and, if you got in good with Rufus, the bartender, you could drink on a tab. We were drinking too much and working too much and living in this Cuba Town bubble. I would watch TV sometimes and see these sitcoms, like *Friends*, and marvel at the ordinariness of their lives. How does one live this kind of slick and easy life? I'd wonder. I was nearly twenty, I could drink illegally in every bar in Cuba Town, and I was already tired. Life seemed harder than it ought to be. I still had that hollow feeling, but now I was haggard as well. I felt too old for my age.

One day Garth was in town and things happened that, though I didn't get it at the time, set my life whirling into a new direction.

I took the weekend off work and Garth stayed with us.

Garth, shirtless, shoeless, in jean shorts, pulled back his long, light-brown hair and put it into a ponytail. He seemed to me like someone else now. I felt like I hardly knew this new Garth.

The air-conditioner hummed on high. "Look at this shit!" said Garth. "This is just ballsy as all hell!" He held up the plastic baggy and slowly lowered it onto the palm of his hand, acted like he was weighing it. "It's like," he paused, "three grams short." It was Sunday and he had some 'business meetings' lined up.

"Save the histrionics and throw me the bag. I'll roll one."

Garth rolled the bag of pot into a thin torpedo and threw it across the table to me. He sat quietly for a few minutes rubbing his hands over his biceps and triceps, watching me deseed the pot. Garth used to be goofy and fun, but now Garth had become almost cocky and, to be honest, a little bit scary. "Not too tight, man. You always roll too tight."

"Whatever. *Es todo bien…*" I licked the adhesive strip on the rolling paper and a small chunk of pot stuck to my tongue.

"Dude, you do. You always do. I'm telling ya. Shit ain't all goddamn good, neither." Garth stopped caressing his arms and moved to his chest. "I'm afraid I'm gonna have to get physical or something with Chris, man," he said calmly. "His nonchalance is getting way out of hand." Chris was this local guy who he'd been fronting pot and acid to.

I held up my definitely-not-too-tightly-rolled joint and admire it. Chris, this local guy, worked with Jessie and we'd hung out with him on occasion. I didn't like him. I was sure no one did.

"Just light it," said Garth.

"Can't say he isn't asking for it." I pulled a red Bic lighter from my jean's pocket and lit the joint. I took a few short drags to get the cherry going and then took one long one.

"I guess, sometimes, I'm *blinded* by my own generosity." Garth grabbed a faded black t-shirt from the back of his chair and put it on. "Pass it, Humphrey," he said.

I leaned across the table and handed him the joint. He examined it, gently rolling it in his fingers. "Man," he said. "It's too tight! What did I fucking say?" He grinned and then hit the joint.

"Actually, I wouldn't mind seeing you kick his ass." I picked up the bag and took in the citrusy smell of its contents. I noticed a few shriveled orange peels in with the pot. "What time is it?"

Garth lobbed me the joint.

"The fuck should I know?"

He stood up, stretched, and walked away, disappearing into the bathroom. I noted how he seemed more comfortable in my apartment than I did. Really he was more comfortable anywhere than I was. This was part of his new way, this possessive, dominant way about him. He acted like he owned everything.

"Five-thirty," he yelled. "When we say we were heading over there?"

"An hour. Come hit this."

When Garth returned to the living room he was wearing mirrored wrap-around Oakley sunglasses and carried his shoes and a pair of greyish socks in one hand. He sat down at the table and grabbed the joint out of my hand.

Garth and I decided to walk to Chris's house instead of taking my car. I now had a dark blue 1983 Buick Regal my dad had bought me on the promise that I would enroll in community college. 'I'll pay the insurance, too, as long as you start school,' he said.

It was a piece of shit, but it got us around. I had been on the fence about college, but I didn't let my dad know that.

Jessie, not long after I got the car, had brought me home a pamphlet from the community college. I'd perused it and thrown it on the coffee table.

"This way we can sneak up on him," said Garth, as I'm locking the front door of our apartment. "Did you know that he owes me twelve hundred dollars? It's unconscionable, man... Fucking unconscionable."

"That's not good business, Garth. You should have known better."

"I'm a trusting soul, is all." He winked. "Two months ago—that last night we all hung out— I fronted him 3 oh-zees of that stuff I got from Mafia Guy—that really good shit with the huge reddish buds. That alone was six hundred, right there. Then two weeks ago, he begged me to front him a sheet of King Elephants. My best acid. I did, and at five hundred for the whole sheet. A fucking steal. Plus, at Keystone last Saturday, I fronted him four rolls so he could impress these rickety, bug-eyed raver chicks. That's a hundred more. He needs to pay me something today. He needs to pay me at least half *today*. Or shit will get ugly."

"I'd say so. I'd also say you need to quit fronting him shit. That's not how you make money."

Once we were two houses away from Chris's place we stopped talking and slowed down. It was just getting dark out. We had to be very quiet. Chris always left his windows open so that he could hear people approaching. This was paranoia, partially because the drugs, but mostly because he was always fucking people over.

It was very humid out. You could hear those little chirping cricket-things going nuts in the hedges around Chris's house. There was a warm, dense breeze. Two grackles hopped across the street.

Garth and I walked up Chris's side yard, as quietly as we could, and I heard some music. We paused for a moment, crouched down next to his living room window.

"Toots and the Maytals," I whispered to Garth. "Good shit."

Garth winked and smiled.

I heard a bubbling sound over the music: someone hitting a water bong. It stopped. Someone coughed and exhaled.

"Yes!" It was Chris's voice. Someone else laughed. Chris started singing the chorus of *Funky Kingston*.

"Watch this," whispered Garth.

"HANDS IN THE AIR, FUCKERS!" he commanded in a deep voice. We both jumped in front of the window.

Chris dropped the water bong, which spilled on the floor, and he leapt over the couch. Garth and I laughed. Chris realized who it was and walked back into the living room. "Fuck, man! Scared the shit out of me."

His brother, Jason, sat on the couch in his bright red Crisp Chix work shirt. He was laughing too. As we stood there, still outside the window, a tiny blond walked into the living room from the bathroom. She sat down on the love seat and, as if nothing unusual was happening, lit a cigarette. I liked the easy way she moved. She seemed very blasé about the whole scene.

"Why so jumpy, Chris?" Garth said through the window screen, still laughing. "You paranoid about something?"

"What you think, man?"

"We're coming around," said Garth, and we walked around the house to the front door.

***

Garth sat down on the couch next to Chris, and I sat on the

love seat next to the tiny blond. Her hair was short, cut into a bob, and it was almost perfectly white. She just sat there smoking. Her eyes were light blue. What was she doing hanging out with these losers?

"Bum a smoke?" I said.

"Go ahead," she said, pointing to the pack on the coffee table.

I picked up the pack, generics, and shook one out. I put it in my mouth and she lit it for me. I thanked her.

Jason stood up, told us all goodbye and left for work. I never understood how he did it, but he went to work stoned all the time.

"Pack a bowl," Garth said to Chris. It was a demand. He looked around the room with a big, cruel grin on his face. This is going to be fun, I thought.

While Chris packed the bowl Garth did little foreboding things. He grabbed Chris's knee and squeezed it, like a dad would his young son. He patted Chris on the head. At one point he started picking things up off the coffee table and scrutinizing them. Some of the things he put in his pockets. One of the things he took from the coffee table was a small one-hitter pipe that was made to look like a cigarette. "This is nice," he said, and then put it in his front pocket. "You still packing that bowl?"

"It was stemmy," said Chris. "I was just making sure I got all the stems and seeds out, man." He handed the water bong to Garth.

"That's very rigorous of you," said Garth. "We truly appreciate it." He lit the bowl and sucked at the open end of the bong. He took a huge hit and put the bong down on the coffee table. He held the hit in for a long time. The room was quiet. Chris went for the bong and Garth batted his hand away. Chris looked at Garth, still holding in his hit.

"What, man?" said Chris.

Garth exhaled what was left of his hit into Chris's face. "Just playing. Go ahead."

Chris shook his head. He's wearing Chris down, I thought. Chris could hit that bong all day long and wouldn't get high with Garth sitting there next to him.

He took his hit and then passed the bong to me.

I hit it and handed it to the blond, but then pulled it back.

"Don't play games with me," she said.

"I just want to know your name. I can't pass this thing to a nameless face."

"My face isn't nameless," she said. She grabbed the bong. Hit it. Paused. Exhaled. "Jenn," she said.

"Jenn." I looked over at Garth, who was putting something else from Chris's coffee table in his pocket. He winked at me.

Jenn got up and walked the bong over to Garth. Garth stood up and bowed and received the bong. Still standing, he turned and looked at Chris, sitting next to him on the couch.

"Dude, what?" said Chris.

"Where's my money?"

"Come on, Garth," said Chris. "Not now." He motioned his head towards Jenn and me, sitting on the love seat. We both watched, each of us smoking one of her cheap cigarettes.

"Where's my money?" Garth repeated.

"Shouldn't we talk about this in private?" Chris, still sitting on the couch, was nervously putting strands of his long black hair behind his right ear, looking up at Garth's imposing figure standing over him.

Garth reared the bong back behind his head and swung it down on top of Chris's head. There was a deep pop and the bong shattered. Water and glass flew.

I started laughing, so did Jenn.

"Where is my money?" Garth repeated flatly without raising his voice.

"What the fuck, man!" Chris stood up, picking glass out of his hair. "What the fuck!" He didn't appear to be bleeding. "That bong cost me a hundred and twenty bucks, man!"

"That's a shame, dude. Give me my money." Garth's eyes were wide, and he was smiling now.

"How much do you need?" said Chris.

"Need?" Garth looked at me, spat out a laugh. "Can you believe this shit?"

"Wow," I said. I looked at Jenn and we both smiled.

Garth looked back at Chris. He was still holding the base of the jagged pipe. "It's my fucking money, Chris. I don't *need* any of it. Lucky for you, I don't need a goddamn dime of it. I don't ever put myself in needy situations, unlike some people. But it's my money, and I fucking want it."

I'm watching all this in awe, thinking, this is Garth now. He is right at home doing this kind of thing. He thrives on it. He has found his way. Everyone's way isn't college or gainful employment. There are people made for this kind of thing. No wonder he doesn't mind fronting drugs to unreliable people. If he didn't he wouldn't have the opportunity to do this kind of thing.

"All right, man. All right..." Chris shuffled backwards and then turned and jogged into his room. "I'll be right back!" He shouted.

"You fucking better be." Garth put the broken bong down on the coffee table. He looked at me and then at Jenn.

"Who are you?" he said.

Jenn pointed at herself and looked at me.

"She's Jenn," I said.

"I'm Jenn," she said.

Garth said, "Cool…"

When Chris returned he handed Garth a wad of bills.

Garth stood there holding it. "What's this?"

"It's your money."

"Yes, it *is* my money, Christopher Paul Reilly. But," he did the weighing thing with his hand, "it's not all of my money. How much is it?"

"It's three hundred. It's all I got right now."

"That's a *quarter* of what you owe me."

"I know. Sorry, man. It's all I got."

Garth crammed the fist of money into his front jean's pocket. He looked out the window at Chris's shiny black Chevy S-10 parked in the front yard.

"How old's that truck, Chris, a year?"

"Just about… yeah."

"Give me the keys." Garth put out his hand.

"Come on, man." Chris stood next to the coffee table.

"Here's the deal," said Garth. "You still owe me nine hundred dollars. I'm going to drive your nice new truck around until you pay me, in full. Toss me the keys."

Chris lobbed his keys to Garth. "This is not cool, dude."

Garth walked over to Chris and grabbed him by his hair and, with a jerk of his arm, slung him onto the couch and then climbed on top of him, straddled him like a defeated animal. He reached over to the coffee table and picked up the bong and aimed the jagged end of it under Chris' chin.

"I'll tell you what's not cool, shithead—making deals you can't follow through on. Making promises you can't keep. That's *not cool*. You have no idea the type of people I'm dealing with on the other end. You think I'm hardcore? You think I'm a mean motherfucker? The guys I'm dealing with will deform you. Come to think of it, you're actually a lucky guy."

"All right, man, all right! I'm sorry! Just don't cut me with that thing—it's got bong water and shit all over it."

Garth put the bong back on the table and got off Chris. "If you don't have my money by the end of this week, I'm going to seriously mangle you." Garth turned to me. "Come on." He held up Chris' truck keys, jingled them and smiled.

I got up from the love seat.

"You want to come with us?" Garth said to Jenn.

She looked at me and back at Garth. "Uh, sure."

Chris said nothing.

***

When we got back to the apartment, after midnight, Jessie was sleeping on the couch, a cigarette still smoked in the ashtray. Garth and Jenn hesitated at the door.

"Dude, I don't want to wake her," said Garth. "I think I'll take Jenn home in my new truck."

I tiptoed to the fridge and grabbed a beer. I sat down in a chair by the entrance to our small kitchen. I smoked and drank and watched Jessie sleep from across the room. She was curled up around a pillow, a small fuzzy blanket over her legs. I thought about us, wondered how we ended up together in the first place and how long we'd stay together. It was clear to me that these kinds of things didn't last. Everyone says so. I said to myself, "One day she's going to leave you." The thought made me sad, but not that sad. I felt, in that moment, that life was very long, not short like everyone says, and that I was worn down—not quite twenty-one, tired and sick.

I glanced over at the community college pamphlet on

the coffee table and thought about picking it up, but didn't. Maybe later, I thought. Maybe tomorrow.

I got up and walked to the fridge for another beer, and on my way back to my chair I watched Jessie roll off the couch. I ran over to her.

She lay there on the floor blinking her eyes slowly.

"You fell off the couch!" I held out my hand and she took it and I pulled her up onto the couch. She was so small, like a child.

"I was dreaming." She sat up straight and stretched her arms and torso.

"You okay? You need anything?"

"I'm okay," she said. "I just forgot...something."

She yawned, grabbed her pack of cigarettes from the coffee table.

"Was it a bad dream?" I lit her cigarette.

"No," she exhaled a burst of smoke. "It wasn't. It was... I don't know... very real."

I took a sip of beer and then put the bottle on the table.

"What was it about?"

"I can't remember. It was one of those ones that seems so real, like you don't know you're sleeping."

"I know what you mean." I looked at the TV and saw our dim gray reflection in it. "Can I ask you something?"

She looked at me and furrowed her brow. Her face, around her eyes, was puffy, and her hair on one side was all pushed up from sleeping on it. "I don't know, what?"

"It's nothing. I was just wondering. How did we end up together? I feel like it all happened so fast. I feel like no decisions were made. We just ended up here...now."

She fidgeted and scooted deeper into the couch, sighed. "You make us sound like an old couple."

"Forget it. I just know you could have gone with just

about anybody. Garth was an obvious choice."

"I knew you would never hurt me, I guess. I knew you'd let me be me. Not like Garth. He scares me. There's something unpredictable about him—like a wild animal. You're kind and gentle, I guess."

"A thoughtful answer to a difficult question," I said. "Garth wasn't always like that, you know—scary."

She tamped out her cigarette, ignoring what I'd said in response. "Man," she said, "that dream."

"It's strange, you know, how something can go from seeming so real to your not being able to remember it at all."

She made a face like she was thinking, then she said, "Give me some of that," and reached for my beer.

I handed it to her and she took a long sip.

"That's good," she said. She took another sip.

"Keep it," I said. "I'm done." The words almost had an echo in the tiny apartment. I glanced out the front window. We had no streetlight, so it was very dark outside.

She smiled and pulled at my shirt. "I'm so tired," she said. She leaned into me, and put her arms around me. "I feel like an old lady," she said.

I closed my eyes and brought her closer.

Acknowledgements

Thanks to Tim Dodd and Matt Phillips, for inspiration and friendship. A massive thanks to George Singleton for his unprovoked kindness and generosity. Thanks to Adam Van Winkle who, during a very busy time in his life, gave a hand. Many thanks due, finally, to Craig Douglas for his patience, generosity, and expertise. Pints all around...

Made in the USA
Columbia, SC
05 July 2021

41432623R00128